"They're all over the place."

Captain Greenbriar heard the thud of heavy footfalls from somewhere down the corridor. He saw Grolsch and his fellow survivors exchange looks.

"We've got to get out of here."

Grolsch turned to Greenbriar. "Sir?"

It was then that the captain realized he wasn't going to win this one. The odds were stacked too high against him. It was just a matter of time before the aliens overran his ship.

The realization changed things. He no longer hoped to contain the invaders. His goal now was to get a message out to Starfleet—to let them know what had happened to the *Cochise,* so they could formulate some kind of plan.

Because if the aliens could do this to *his* ship, they could do it to a hundred others.

Other *Stargazer* Novels

The Valiant
Gauntlet
Progenitor
Three
Oblivion

Requiem
Reunion
First Virtue

STAR TREK®

S T A R G A Z E R
ENIGMA

Michael Jan Friedman

Based upon
Star Trek: The Next Generation®
created by Gene Roddenberry

POCKET BOOKS
New York   London   Toronto   Sydney

An *Original* Publication of POCKET BOOKS

POCKET BOOKS, a division of Simon & Schuster, Inc.
1230 Avenue of the Americas, New York, NY 10020

STAR TREK is a Registered Trademark of Paramount Pictures.

This book is published by Pocket Books, a division of Simon & Schuster, Inc., under exclusive license from Paramount Pictures.

ISBN: 978-1-4516-4635-1

First Pocket Books printing August 2004

10 9 8 7 6 5 4 3 2 1

POCKET and colophon are registered trademarks of Simon & Schuster, Inc.

Manufactured in the United States of America

For information regarding special discounts for bulk purchases, please contact Simon & Schuster Special Sales at 1-800-456-6798 or business@simonandschuster.com

For Julius Schwartz

STARGAZER
ENIGMA

Chapter One

As Jean-Luc Picard made his way down the long, curving corridor on his way to Transporter Room One, he saw Lieutenant Urajel coming from the other direction.

"Lieutenant," he said, favoring the Andorian with a nod.

"Captain," she returned.

But she wasn't looking him in the eye. She was looking at his head—a common problem of late, as he had been compelled to shave it weeks ago in a place called Oblivion, and his hair was growing back more slowly than anyone had expected.

At the moment, it was little more than stubble, and itchy stubble at that. Rather a nuisance all around, the captain reflected, as he passed Urajel and continued on his way.

Unfortunately, his hair was the least of his problems.

At the end of the corridor, he found a set of double doors, which hissed open at his approach. Beyond them, two of his people were waiting for him.

No, he thought, amending his observation. *Just one of them is still mine.*

That was Goetz, the red-haired junior operator on duty in the ship's primary transporter room. She was standing behind the enclosure's lone control console, awaiting the captain's authorization to proceed.

The other figure in the room—the one who was no longer Picard's to command—was standing on the slightly raised transporter platform, dressed in a brown tunic with gray pants and a shirt of the same color. He had left all his cranberry-and-black Starfleet uniforms hanging in his quarters, as it was no longer appropriate for him to wear any of them.

Picard met the man's eyes. "Mister Nikolas," he said.

The ensign—no, the captain reminded himself, *former* ensign—inclined his head. "Captain."

Andreas Nikolas appeared relieved, as if a great weight had been lifted from his shoulders. And no doubt it had been. A couple of days earlier, he had come to Picard with a haunted, hollowed-out look in his eyes—the same look the captain had seen lurking there for the last several weeks.

Ever since Gerda Idun Asmund had left them.

She had arrived on the *Stargazer* in an apparent transporter accident, one that had shot her from her original timeline into Picard's own. As it turned out later, her transit was actually part of an elaborate plan

2

to kidnap Phigus Simenon, the *Stargazer*'s chief engineer, and put him to work for a rebel cause.

Gerda Idun was foiled—with Nikolas's help, as fate would have it—and she was returned to her proper universe empty-handed. But that was only after Nikolas had done himself the disservice of falling in love with her.

From that point on, the ensign's life on the *Stargazer* had been a little bit of hell. After all, Gerda and Idun Asmund, who looked exactly like Gerda Idun, were still serving alongside him on the ship. And every time Nikolas bumped into one of them, in a corridor or a lounge, he was painfully reminded of what he had lost.

Picard had been aware of Nikolas's discomfort. However, he had assumed that Nikolas would get over it, as Picard had gotten over his own lost loves. So he was surprised when the fellow walked into the captain's ready room a few days ago, sat down opposite him, and asked for his discharge from Starfleet.

Picard was torn by the request. Ever since Nikolas had beamed aboard the *Stargazer,* the captain had identified with him and seen promise in him.

Nikolas had been reprimanded a few times for getting into fights, that was true. But Picard had his share of ill-considered dust-offs at that age, and he had eventually grown past them. He had seen no reason why Nikolas couldn't do the same.

Then Gerda Idun had appeared, and Nikolas changed. The day she was slated to leave, his orders called for him to report to engineering. Instead, he went to the transporter room from which she was departing, determined to speak with her.

And days later, after the captain had specifically warned Nikolas about getting into any more fights with his fellow crewmen, he had managed to get into not one such conflict, but *two*—both of them with Lieutenant Hanta, who should have known better as well.

Picard had considered the idea of encouraging Nikolas to transfer to another ship. However, that would have solved only a portion of the fellow's problem. Even if Nikolas had been removed from the presence of the Asmund twins, he would still have been distracted by his memories of Gerda Idun.

And an officer on a starship couldn't afford such a distraction. Not when it might place his colleagues in deadly danger.

Finally—feeling he had no choice in the matter—the captain had given in. He had approved Nikolas's resignation from the fleet. But he had done so with a heavy heart.

Under normal circumstances, Nikolas would have been compelled to remain on the *Stargazer* for weeks. It usually took that long to arrange a series of handoffs with other starships in the transport of a low-priority passenger.

However, there had been a change in Picard's orders, requiring him to go halfway back to Earth. That had drastically expedited Nikolas's departure—bringing about this day, this time, and this unfortunate moment.

Standing there alongside Goetz, the captain considered Nikolas for a moment. He couldn't help feeling that he had failed somehow—that he had let the younger man down, rather than the other way around.

No matter how one looked at the situation, it was a shame. Picard turned to his transporter operator.

"Is the *Manitou* ready?" he asked, referring to the ship with which they had rendezvoused minutes earlier.

Goetz nodded. "She is, sir."

Picard turned to his former ensign and said, "I wish you well, Mister Nikolas."

Nikolas's brow knit, as if he were feeling a pang of regret. Or maybe it was simply an indication of how impatient he was to be off the *Stargazer.*

Finally, he said, "The same to you, sir."

The captain acknowledged the gesture with a nod. Then he glanced at Goetz and said, "Energize."

Picard watched a column of golden light take shape around Nikolas, immersing him in its brilliance. After a moment, he began to fade away. Little by little, his features became indistinguishable from the light.

Then the light faded too, leaving nothing in its place.

Picard sighed. But it wasn't just Nikolas's departure that compelled him to do so. After all, the *Stargazer* was slated to *receive* a transport subject as well as give one up.

Goetz turned to the captain. "Sir, Nikolas has arrived safely on the *Manitou.*"

Picard nodded. "Proceed."

This time, the transporter operator didn't have much to do, as her opposite number on the *Manitou* was the one initiating the transport. Goetz's only responsibility was to give the other ship's operator the go-ahead, which she did with a tap on her console, and then monitor the procedure.

Seconds later, another column of golden light took shape on the platform. As Picard looked on, it became clear that there was someone forming inside it—someone obviously humanoid, who solidified as the splendor around him vanished.

He was blond, of medium build, and older than the captain by a couple of decades. Though he was wearing the same cranberry and black uniform, the insignia on it denoted a rank superior to Picard's—that of the Starfleet admiral overseeing this sector of space.

McAteer, thought the captain, and not with any special fondness. But what he said was "Admiral. Welcome to the *Stargazer.*"

McAteer smiled as if he were happy to see Picard, but his smile wasn't to be taken at face value. It was merely a tool that he used to disarm his adversaries.

"Picard," he said as he stepped down from the platform.

Not *Captain* Picard. Just *Picard,* without the title. But then, McAteer had never seemed comfortable with the notion of someone Picard's age commanding a starship.

"You've cut your hair," the admiral observed.

"I did," the captain confirmed. "A necessary part of my assignment on Oblivion."

"Ah yes," said McAteer. "Oblivion." As if that single word were comment enough.

Picard's mission there hadn't been a complete success. He had, after all, failed to obtain strategic information that would have given the Federation a significant advantage over its adversaries in the sector.

However, he had flushed out a scheme to put the

Federation at a significant *dis*advantage. Most superior officers would have taken that into consideration. But not McAteer.

"I trust your trip here was a comfortable one," said the captain.

"It was," the admiral confirmed. "But then, Captain Dorchester knows his way around."

And I don't, Picard couldn't help adding silently. The implication was there whether McAteer said it out loud or not.

The captain indicated the exit. "Shall I have someone see you to your quarters?"

"Not just yet," said McAteer. "Right now, I'd like to go over a few things in your ready room."

Of course you would, thought Picard.

Carter Greyhorse, the *Stargazer*'s chief medical officer, appeared to be studying the red-on-black digital readout on the side of one of his biobeds. However, he was really thinking about Gerda Asmund. In point of fact, he was *always* thinking about Gerda Asmund.

And why not? She was his lover.

Greyhorse had never imagined he would be saying such a thing, not even to himself. But it was true. The fates had been kinder to him than he could ever have imagined. Lovely, fierce Gerda had miraculously seen fit to share his bed.

And not *just* his bed.

After all, Gerda had been raised as a Klingon. Her appetites were untidy, to say the least, and they had a way of manifesting themselves even when there was no bed available.

More than once in recent weeks, Greyhorse had found himself in a semipublic part of the ship, hastily covering up some newly inflicted wound—the livid result of Gerda's passion. He was sporting two such wounds at that very moment, one half-healed and the other still fresh and bloody.

The doctor didn't like the risks he and Gerda were taking, sometimes getting involved with each other while one or both of them were on duty. However, his lover seemed to thrive on risk. For her, it appeared to be an integral part of the experience.

He couldn't deny her that thrill. Hell, he couldn't deny her *anything*—not when Gerda might suddenly decide that Greyhorse was too much trouble and end their relationship, just like that. He didn't know how he would go on living if she did that.

So he endured their trysts, no matter where or when they took place, and the scars that came with them, and still he counted himself lucky. And he would go on doing that as long as Gerda gave him the chance to—

"Doctor?" said his patient, interrupting Greyhorse's thoughts.

He looked down at Ulelo, one of the com officers who reported to Lieutenant Paxton. "Yes?"

"Have you got everything you needed?"

Greyhorse nodded. "Yes. Yes, of course. You can go."

He should have scrutinized Ulelo's bioscan, just to be certain there was nothing wrong with the man. However, a cursory look hadn't given him any reason for concern, and he would take a closer look at the scan later on.

Besides, Ulelo hadn't had any complaints. It was just a routine checkup, mandated by Starfleet regulations.

"Thank you," said the com officer.

"No problem," said Greyhorse.

Swiveling himself around and removing himself from the biobed, Ulelo crossed sickbay and headed for the exit. By the time the doctor heard the clatter of Ulelo's footfalls in the corridor outside, he wasn't thinking about the com officer anymore.

He was thinking about Gerda again.

Chapter Two

PICARD REGARDED ADMIRAL MCATEER across the shiny black surface of his desk. The admiral, who was scanning the captain's ready room for the first time, looked faintly disapproving.

"Is that a dictionary?" asked McAteer, referring to a hardbound book lying on a side table next to a bulkhead.

"No," said Picard, "though I can understand how you might have come to that conclusion. It is an illustrated volume of the complete works of William Shakespeare."

McAteer made a face. "Shakespeare, eh?"

"Yes," said the captain. "I gather you are not especially fond of the man's work."

"I saw a production of *Henry the Fifth* back in San Francisco," the admiral explained. "I didn't love it."

"Sorry to hear it," Picard remarked.

"Not as sorry as I was," said McAteer, clearly not above chuckling at his own quip.

The captain chuckled too, if only to be polite.

For a moment, silence gathered between Picard and his guest like storm clouds on a hot summer evening. It emphasized that, despite their small talk about Shakespeare, they were not even remotely bound by bonds of friendship.

Finally, McAteer spoke again. "As you may have guessed," he said, "I've got an assignment for you."

Had those words come from anyone else in an admiral's uniform, Picard would have been intrigued by them. But this was McAteer, a man who had repeatedly demonstrated an inclination to give the *Stargazer* the least important missions in the fleet.

"An assignment?" the captain echoed.

"Yes." McAteer leaned back in his chair. "I take it you're familiar with the Delta Campara system?"

Picard felt the muscles in his jaw ripple, but he otherwise contained his emotions. "I am."

Delta Campara was a Cepheid variable star, a rather large and unstable body given to violent bursts of energy at irregular and therefore unexpected intervals. Picard had seen a few such stars in the course of his Academy missions, though none as big or volatile as Delta Campara.

"I'd like you to take a look at it," said the admiral, "and see what kinds of changes it's undergone since the *Excelsior* surveyed it a quarter of a century ago."

Picard frowned. Under different circumstances, he wouldn't have minded the idea of a survey. He was as intrigued by stellar phenomena as any captain in the fleet.

But there were more pressing concerns in the sector than a star that had been scanned just twenty-five years earlier. More and more, there were controversies arising from the Ubarrak and the Cardassians. And as always, it seemed the *Stargazer* was being left out of them.

"Should be interesting," said McAteer.

It would have been politic to agree. Instead Picard said, "Permission to speak freely, sir?"

"Are you sure?" Ensign Cole Paris asked.

"I am," said Jiterica, using the tinny, artificial voice granted her by her specially designed containment suit.

Paris looked into her eyes—or rather, the illusion of eyes that Jiterica had created for herself behind her helmet's transparent faceplate. She looked back at him unflinchingly, without even a hint of uncertainty.

Even a week earlier, he might not have relied on Jiterica's expression as an accurate barometer of her Nizhrak feelings. But she had gotten so good at mimicking human reactions, he allowed himself to be reassured by it.

After all, it was a big step they were taking. He didn't want to rush it and ruin everything. But at the same time, he could barely wait. His pulse was already racing in anticipation.

"Ready?" asked Jiterica.

What a question. "Hell, yes," he said.

Taking that as her cue, Jiterica reached up with the gloves of her containment suit and started unfastening her helmet. Her manual dexterity still left something to be desired, so it wasn't as smooth a process as it could have been.

"Do you need help?" Paris asked.

"No," said Jiterica. "I can manage it."

It took her a while, but she finally released the latch and pushed back her helmet. The act exposed her ghostly head, which tilted ever so slightly as she returned Paris's gaze. For a heartbeat or two, Jiterica remained in her vaguely humanoid shape, even without the help of the suit's built-in containment field. Then her features twisted away like smoke in a strong breeze, and the suit dropped precipitously to the floor.

But there was a cloud looming over it, a gradually expanding complex of shifting, sparkling particles, which was no less the essence of Jiterica than what had been squeezed into the suit. If anything, the cloud was *more* her, because she was allowing herself to revert to her natural state—that of a low-density being whose species had evolved in the chaotic upper atmosphere of a high-gravity gas giant.

As Paris watched, spellbound, Jiterica grew to fill the confines of her quarters—and they truly *were* confines, because she could have easily filled a larger space. But compared with the compression she had endured in her suit, the chance to fill even a modest compartment had to seem like a great relief.

As Jiterica encompassed Paris, taking him inside herself, he could feel her alien touch—first on the exposed skin of his face, neck, and hands, and then all over his body. It reached him right through the fabric of his clothes, cold and sharp as any needle, as if he were standing naked in a shower of ice shards.

Then he heard Jiterica speak to him, not in the suit's mechanical voice but in a language without sound. And it wasn't a mouth she was speaking with, but every energy-charged molecule of her body.

Closing his eyes, he allowed himself to hear every word, every sensation, every sentiment. He breathed her in, exhaled, and breathed her in again.

Like fairy dust, Paris thought. Like a deeply intoxicating liqueur, except it was alive and intelligent and basking in an array of unheard-of emotions.

Beautiful, exquisite emotions. The kind he hadn't imagined he would ever know.

But it wasn't just the intoxication, or the novelty, or the sense of joining that Paris loved. It was the fact that Jiterica was part of it. With some other Nizhrak the experience might still have been an appealing one, but it was Jiterica who took his breath away.

It was bliss, complete and utter bliss. And somehow, Paris knew that Jiterica felt the same way.

For what seemed like a long time, he drifted on the electric pleasure of her currents, immersed and immersing, embracing and embraced. Then, with a pang of deep regret, Paris felt Jiterica stir as if to withdraw.

Don't, he thought.

But she gave him the sense that she needed to—that they *both* needed to. So Paris opened his eyes and watched her go.

He was still in touch with her, if not quite as intimately as before, when she began to force herself back into her containment suit. He had known that it was difficult for her to compress, but he had never appreciated *how* difficult.

First, Jiterica filled up the suit's arms and legs, so she would have use of them. Then, with what seemed like an intense effort, she used the gloves to pull her helmet back into place.

As before, Paris was moved to help her, but he could tell that she wanted to do this herself. She had worked hard to gain whatever modicum of dexterity she possessed, and she was determined to put it to use.

Finally, Jiterica closed the helmet latches and turned to him. But her face hadn't quite coalesced yet. It was still crude, lacking in definition.

Then she took care of that detail as well. Her features clarified, sharpened, became familiar to him.

Only then did Paris ask the question that had been nagging at him: "Why did we need to stop?"

Jiterica smiled. "It's time," she said in her artificial voice, "for our next shift."

"No . . ." said Paris.

He couldn't believe it. They had just completed their *last* shift when they met in Jiterica's quarters. Was it possible that they had been there for *sixteen hours?*

He had barely considered the possibility when he felt the encroaching emptiness in his belly, and the thirst, and an unusual stiffness in his legs. And by those signs, he knew that Jiterica wasn't kidding.

Sixteen hours, the ensign thought, as he smiled back at her. *Amazing.*

* * *

Gilaad Ben Zoma, first officer of the *Stargazer* and incidentally Jean-Luc Picard's best friend, had been trying for the last minute or so to concentrate his attention on the oval-shaped data-display device in his hand.

Unfortunately, he wasn't doing a very good job of it. And that wasn't likely to change while Admiral McAteer and the captain were holed up in Picard's ready room.

"They've been in there a long time," observed Elizabeth Wu, the ship's highly efficient second officer, who had handed Ben Zoma the data-display device in the first place.

He nodded. "They certainly have. I guess they've got something . . . complicated to talk about."

"Think it's a mission?" Wu asked.

Ben Zoma smiled a little. "More than that. Starfleet admirals—even those as intrusive as McAteer—don't come out this far just to give an order. Something's up."

Wu frowned. "Something we're not going to like, I take it?"

The first officer stared at the ready-room door as if he could see through it. "I don't doubt it."

Picard had kept his mouth shut for a good long time, but he could keep it shut no longer—which was why he had petitioned his superior for permission to speak freely, unfettered by the restricting bonds of Starfleet protocol.

On the other side of the captain's desk, McAteer's eyes narrowed almost imperceptibly. But he didn't take long to consider the request. "Granted."

Picard plunged ahead. "There is a tempest brewing in this sector, Admiral. You know that as well as anyone."

McAteer didn't disagree.

"In your place," Picard continued, "I would be deploying the entirety of my resources to address the situation at hand. And yet, with the notable exception of my assignment on Oblivion, in which my involvement was mandated by parties other than yourself, you have consistently relegated the *Stargazer* to peripheral activities. While other *Constellation*-class vessels serve as escorts through disputed territory or conduct border patrols, *my* vessel carries out scientific surveys—and frivolous ones at that."

The captain leaned forward in his chair. "My crew is ready, willing, and able to handle any crisis that may arise, be it diplomatic or military in nature. We are eager to make the same sort of contributions as any other ship in the fleet—to do the same work and assume the same risks—and we would be grateful if you recognized that fact."

McAteer smiled through Picard's diatribe, apparently without resentment. Then, taking his time, he answered the captain's challenge.

"You say that your crew is equal to any task I may decide to impose upon it. That may be so," said McAteer. "However, to be perfectly blunt, its commanding officer appears *not* to be equal to any task."

Picard felt as if he had been slapped across the face.

"That," the admiral continued, in an even, almost benevolent-sounding tone, "is the reason I've been reluctant to put the *Stargazer* in the thick of the action— because your personal performance hasn't earned my confidence."

The captain bit his lip to keep from saying something he would certainly regret. If McAteer wasn't confident in him, it wasn't his fault. He had done everything the man had asked of him, and a good deal more.

His only mistake had been his choice of birthdate. In the admiral's estimate, Picard was too young to be a captain, too inexperienced, too green.

"And that," said McAteer, looking as if he were allowing himself to be dragged into unplanned but all-too-necessary territory, "is also why I have scheduled a hearing to judge your competence as a Starfleet captain."

Picard felt his cheeks suffuse with blood. "My *competence?*" he echoed, giving the word an ironic spin. "And in what respect have I been incompetent?"

Without a second's hesitation, the admiral reeled off a list of instances. Bad decisions, he called them, constructed on the uncertain ground of bad judgment.

And they all had to do with the Nuyyad, the conqueror species with whom the *Stargazer* had clashed on the other side of the galactic barrier. Picard had barely taken the reins of command at the time, assuming the place of his dead captain as the enemy slashed away at the *Stargazer.*

But there was no mention of mitigating circumstances, no nod to the novelty of the situation. All McAteer cared to talk about were the specific moves Picard had made.

Taken out of context, each one made the captain sound more careless and devoid of judgment than the one before it. But every one of them had been made for a good reason.

Picard said so.

"Those who serve with you disagree," said the admiral.

Picard was skeptical about that claim, to say the least. He couldn't imagine that Ben Zoma or Wu had ever spoken to McAteer behind his back. *Then who . . . ?*

The admiral's smile deepened. *"Former* colleagues, to be precise. Commander Leach, for instance—Commander Ben Zoma's predecessor as first officer of the *Stargazer.* He provided me with some rather valuable insights into your activities as the *Stargazer'*s second officer. Then there was Ensign Joe Caber—"

The captain couldn't help but interrupt. "Ensign Caber was not Starfleet material, as my report on the reason for his transfer clearly indicated."

"I read it," said McAteer. "You said he was guilty of bigotry toward one of your other crewmen."

"Bigotry that quickly accelerated into unwarranted violence."

"So you said in your report," the admiral noted. "But Ensign Caber had a different take on his stay here."

Why am I not surprised? Caber, the son of a highly regarded Starfleet admiral, had suggested as he left the *Stargazer* that the matter of his dismissal would not be resolved to Picard's satisfaction.

"As you might expect," said McAteer, "Ensign Caber's father has taken a personal interest in your actions. He has asked to be one of the admirals who hear the charges against you."

Perfect, thought the captain.

Clearly, McAteer had gone to a great deal of trouble

to build and fortify his position. He wasn't going to stop at anything to see Picard relieved of his command.

The admiral sighed audibly. "I hope you know I don't like doing this. I don't enjoy raking people over the coals."

Again, Picard bit his lip. Thanks to one of his friends in Starfleet, he knew that McAteer was lying. He had it in for Picard ever since Admiral Mehdi placed the twenty-eight-year old in command of the *Stargazer.*

"Of course," the admiral added in a repulsively avuncular way, "you *could* simply step down. That would save everyone a lot of trouble—*you* in particular."

Picard felt his teeth grind together. *You would like me to think so, wouldn't you?*

"I appreciate the offer," he forced himself to say, "but frankly, I do not intend to give up my command without a fight." He speared McAteer with his gaze. "I ask you—what self-respecting captain *would?*"

The admiral's eyes crinkled at the corners. "As you wish, Picard." He got up and straightened his jacket. "If you happen to change your mind, you know where to find me."

"Indeed," said the captain.

Chapter Three

BEN ZOMA HAD SELDOM seen his friend Picard look so red-faced with subdued anger. He couldn't see the captain's hands, but he imagined that Picard's knuckles were white as they grasped the rests of his desk chair. Obviously, he had been set off by something the admiral had told him.

"So," the first officer opened as he sat down in the chair McAteer had occupied, "what did our friend the admiral have to say that couldn't have been said at a much greater distance and a good deal more succinctly?"

Picard told him.

Ben Zoma usually made light of the captain's concerns. He didn't make light of this one. "The bastard."

"I shouldn't have been surprised," said Picard. "He has never made a secret of his disdain for me."

Ben Zoma frowned. "You just didn't know when he

would pull the rug out. It was something we always figured would happen someday—just not *today.*"

Picard shook his head, no doubt wondering how he had come to this pass. "Perhaps my father was right when he advised me to remain on Earth and run the family vineyard. I understand that last year's vintage, the thirty-two, was the best we ever produced."

The first officer, too, had a father who had opposed his choice to serve in Starfleet. If anyone understood the captain's situation, it was he.

"Don't worry," he said, searching for something comforting to say. "You'll get through this."

"And if I lose the *Stargazer?*" the captain asked, introducing an unwelcome dose of reality. "If McAteer pries me away from her?"

Ben Zoma felt his friend's pain, and wished it were his instead. "That's beyond your control at this point."

Picard sat back in his seat, looking defeated already. "I was hoping you would assure me to the contrary, Gilaad."

Ben Zoma smiled, but there wasn't any mirth in it. "Believe me, I wish I could."

Lieutenant Obal pushed around the green and orange food on his plate, only vaguely aware of the buzz of conversation around him. In the few months he had served on the *Stargazer,* he had spent some eminently enjoyable moments in the mess hall.

This wasn't one of them.

"It's disappointing," Obal's companion said unexpectedly.

Roused from his melancholy, the security officer looked across the table at Kastiigan, the ship's science officer. A Kandilkari, Kastiigan had a long and striated face, with distinctive purple jowls hanging loosely from his jaw.

"What is?" Obal asked.

"Several weeks have passed since I arrived on this vessel," said Kastiigan, "and in that time, various officers have been exposed to considerable danger. But I have not been one of them."

Obal looked at him, more than a little surprised. "You *wish* to be placed in danger?"

The science officer nodded. "Very much so. I am a senior officer on this starship. I should be assuming as much of the risk as any other senior officer."

The Binderian tilted his head. "That is . . . an unusual way of looking at it."

Kastiigan didn't appear to have heard him. He seemed too intent on his own thoughts. "I have made it clear to Captain Picard that I would like to be placed in jeopardy, but for some reason he seems unwilling to do so."

"Perhaps he values your services too much to contemplate losing you," Obal suggested.

The Kandilkari shook his head. "If that's so, he has given me no indication of it."

"Also," the security officer observed, "science officers aren't often exposed to perilous conditions. At least, not as often as other personnel."

It was true. Science officers weren't sent on the ship's most dangerous missions because their skill sets weren't often needed. When science officers were injured or killed on away assignments, it was because their vessel had encountered something unexpected— and ultimately harmful.

"Then perhaps I made a mistake when I became a science officer," Kastiigan concluded. He didn't sound very happy.

Of course, Obal wasn't very happy these days either. But it had nothing to do with how often the captain had placed him in the line of fire.

Ensign Nikolas had been his best friend on the ship. Now that Nikolas had resigned from the fleet and left the *Stargazer,* life would never again be the same for Obal.

Paris and some of the other crewmen had already made attempts to fill the breach, and Obal greatly appreciated their kindness. But none of them was Nikolas.

Naturally, the Binderian didn't mention any of that to Lieutenant Kastiigan. Considering the depth of the science officer's anxiety, it seemed rude to Obal to mention his own.

So he just listened to Kastiigan, and nodded sympathetically, and kept his feelings about Nikolas to himself.

Just a few minutes longer, Picard assured himself, as he watched Admiral McAteer spoon the last blood-red dollop of cherries jubilee into his mouth.

It had been a *most* wearisome day.

The morning had been filled with section meetings, which McAteer had—of course—insisted on attending. First engineering, then sciences, then security, all the way down the line.

Each section head had been grilled up, down, and

sideways until the admiral was satisfied with the answers he received, and then grilled some more. It had been neither pretty nor productive, in the captain's estimate.

But all along, Picard had known that his section heads weren't McAteer's targets. The admiral's only real target was the captain himself; whatever "problems" McAteer found on the *Stargazer,* they would be pinned on Picard and Picard alone.

The afternoon had been even worse. McAteer had taken Picard, Ben Zoma, and Wu down to the observation lounge, and conducted a review of virtually every decision the command staff had made in the last couple of weeks—in other words, since the last subspace data packet received by Starfleet Command.

Neither the captain nor his officers had uttered a word of protest. They had answered all the admiral's questions as if they had some sort of merit, following McAteer through exacting analyses of what were patently procedural minutiae.

Finally, they had sat down to dinner with the admiral—just Picard, Ben Zoma, and Greyhorse, because the other senior officers had work to do—and listened to him describe the high points of his career. There were a great many, apparently.

And through it all, Picard had felt compelled to pretend he wasn't offended by McAteer—by the admiral's opinion of him, by the admiral's very presence here. He had been forced to act as if McAteer were welcome.

A most wearisome day indeed. And the captain expected more of the same the following morning.

"Have you made a decision," he inquired hopefully, while McAteer wiped a bit of cherry debris from his chin, "as to the next stop on your tour?"

The admiral had indicated that he would be visiting several vessels, not just the *Stargazer*. After all, Arlen McAteer was nothing if not "hands-on."

"I'll be going to the *Antares*," the admiral said, picking up his cloth napkin and wiping his mouth. "Captain Vayishra's ship."

Picard knew quite well whose ship it was. So did anyone else who had spent any time with McAteer. As far as the admiral was concerned, there was no finer commanding officer in the fleet than the much-decorated Vayishra.

"Shall I have my com officer contact the *Antares*," Picard suggested, "and arrange a rendezvous?"

McAteer dismissed the idea with a wave of his hand. "That won't be necessary. I don't want to tie up an entire starship when a shuttle will do just fine."

Picard frowned. If McAteer meant to take a shuttle, the captain would have to supply personnel to man it— not just a pilot, but a squad of security officers as well. This was, after all, a Starfleet admiral they would be transporting.

"You're certain?" the captain asked, extending McAteer a chance to reconsider.

"Quite certain," said the admiral, giving him little choice in the matter.

Picard looked up at the intercom grid hidden in the ceiling. "Mister Chang, this is the captain."

"Chang here," came the response.

"Prepare a personnel shuttle for Admiral McAteer

ENIGMA

and a security escort. The admiral will want to leave . . ." He turned to McAteer, leaving it to him to supply the rest of the information.

"Twelve hundred hours tomorrow," said McAteer.

"Consider it done, sir," said the shuttlebay officer. "Chang out."

"Excellent," said the admiral. "Oh, and Picard . . . ?"

The captain turned to him. "Yes?"

"I'd like Paris to pilot the shuttle. That way I'll know I'm in good hands."

Cole Paris *had* distinguished himself as an excellent helm officer. However, Picard suspected that the ensign's lineage, as the scion of an old Starfleet family, had as much to do with McAteer's request as anything else.

The admiral seemed to like people whose families were associated with the fleet. Maybe that was how he had gotten friendly with Admiral Caber.

"Paris it is," Picard assured the admiral. *Anything to get you off this ship.*

Phigus Simenon, chief engineer of the *Stargazer*, cast a critical eye over the console screen in front of him.

Normally, it played host to operating data on any number of ship's systems, from warp drive to waste recycling. Or else it displayed some complicated set of calculations, which no one but Simenon would even consider following without the assistance of a computer.

But at the moment, the engineer's screen was filled with something else—images of a half-dozen lizardlike creatures, their oversized golden eyes peering at him innocently from the safety of their artificial nest.

27

My children, he thought.

It didn't sound right. It didn't *feel* right. And yet, there they were, irrefutable proof that Simenon had indeed made a contribution to the future of his species.

Soon, the hatchlings would be removed from their nest and given to their mother to raise. Simenon hadn't met her, but he had heard good things about her. She would be a fine parent. The children would be trained in the ways of Gnalish society and educated in accordance with their natural talents.

And Simenon? He would do what males of his species had always done. He would stay as far away as possible, minimizing the chances of his screwing everything up.

He recalled his own mother—a stern individual who had taken no guff from anyone, especially her offspring. Now there was a *parent.* He still thought of her on occasion, though he would never have let any of his crewmates know that.

Simenon could just imagine the comments—especially from the humans aboard, who seemed to have a very different relationship with their mothers than his own people did. But then, what could one expect from a species that insisted on feeding its young with maternal secretions?

It made him shiver down to the tip of his scaly tail just thinking about it. He was still doing so when he noticed that he had unaccustomed company—in the large, blue form of Vigo, the *Stargazer*'s weapons officer.

Along with the captain, Ben Zoma, and Doctor Greyhorse, Vigo had earned Simenon's undying gratitude by assisting him in a grueling ritual back on the

Gnalish homeworld. It was that ritual that had ensured Simenon of the progeny pictured on his screen.

At first, the engineer suspected that his colleague had come to challenge him to a game of *sharash'di,* a complex and apparently habit-forming conceit that Vigo had acquired as a gift from another crewman. Then Simenon saw the expression on Vigo's face, and doubted that he had come about a game.

The engineer swiveled in his chair. "What's the matter?"

Vigo grunted softly. "Is it that obvious that I'm troubled?"

"No more obvious than, say, a supernova."

The weapons officer pulled up a chair and sat facing Simenon. "I need to ask you a question," he said.

It wasn't often that crewmates came to the engineer for advice. He just wasn't the type to lend a sympathetic ear. But he gave Vigo's question his full attention.

It wasn't until Vigo was done speaking, and Simenon had seen the light of determinaton in his friend's eyes, that he realized something about the answer he was about to utter. . . .

It was the same as the one already lodged in Vigo's heart.

Hundreds of years earlier, when horse-drawn stagecoaches carried passengers across the middle band of North America called the United States, the man charged with protecting the stagecoach would sit next to the driver.

In his arms, he would cradle a primitive projectile

weapon known as a shotgun. Hence, the derivation of the term "shotgun seat," which referred to the place next to the driver, or pilot, or helmsman of a particular vehicle.

It was this seat that Ben Zoma claimed as soon as he entered the *Livingston,* a sleek, warp-capable person-nel shuttle designed to accommodate a crew of two and six passengers—maximum.

Not that the first officer was so hungry for a view of the stars, which was so eminently available through the vessel's forward observation port. In this case, it was purely a secondary consideration.

It was more a matter of his avoiding Admiral McAteer. By sitting next to the shuttle's primary pilot—Ensign Paris, in this case—Ben Zoma could be certain he wouldn't have to listen to the admiral for the entire trip.

Of course, Paris would eventually turn the helm over to someone else, and Ben Zoma would have to do the same with the shotgun seat. But for the first shift, at least, he knew he would be safe from McAteer's commentary.

"Thanks," he told Chang, the officer in charge of the ship's shuttle deck.

"Don't mention it," said Chang, sticking his head in after Ben Zoma and taking a critical look around. "I just wish my people would be a little neater sometimes."

The first officer inspected the interior of the shuttle. As far as he could tell, it was spotless. He turned to Chang and said, "You're kidding, right?"

Chang looked deadly serious as he regarded Ben Zoma. Then, unexpectedly, he cracked a smile. "Commander, the *Livingston* is the one we *always* keep clean."

Ben Zoma had to laugh. "And they say *I* never take anything seriously."

"The problem," said Chang, "is I take *everything* seriously. If I didn't laugh about it, I'd go insane."

"Pardon me, Lieutenant," said an all-too-familiar voice, "I'd like to board."

Chang cast a glance over his shoulder, then stepped back from the hatch. "Of course, sir."

A moment later, McAteer slid into the *Livingston*. He was halfway inside before he noticed that Ben Zoma had preceded him.

"Well," said the admiral, "we *are* punctual."

"Yes sir, we are," said Ben Zoma.

Fortunately, they didn't have to prolong the conversation, because the rest of the crew arrived in the next few moments. In addition to Paris, it included Chen, Ramirez, Horombo, and Garner—all experienced security officers.

Not that Ben Zoma expected to need them. They were ferrying an admiral from one starship to another, not smuggling tribbles across the heart of the Klingon Empire. However, protocol called for the largest escort possible where such a high-ranking officer was involved, and unless McAteer said otherwise, they were all going to have to pile in.

Before they closed the hatch, Picard appeared. "Bon voyage," he told McAteer, maintaining an air of cordiality. "And please, say hello to Captain Vayishra for me."

If the admiral took note of the sarcasm, he gave no

indication of it. "I'll do that. Thank you for the hospitality, Picard. And," he added, "good luck."

His back to McAteer, Ben Zoma made a face. Good luck was the *last* thing the admiral wanted for Picard.

The captain took a last look around inside the shuttle, briefly meeting his first officer's gaze. Then he nodded to Paris, who used his controls to swing the hatch closed.

Once Picard had withdrawn, the ensign activated the *Livingston*'s thrusters to lift the craft off the deck and bring her about. In a matter of seconds, he and Ben Zoma were facing in the direction of the bay doors. Then the doors parted, revealing the star-pricked blackness of the void.

A semipermeable, transparent barrier kept the air in the bay from rushing out. However, it wouldn't keep the shuttle from doing so. Moving forward, the *Livingston* approached the barrier and the slice of space beyond it.

Then, as smoothly as a bird taking to the sky, the shuttle slid through the aperture. The vast sea of space opened before them, lonely and mysterious.

And they were off.

Chapter Four

DIKEMBE ULELO HAD A JOB to do.

With that idea firmly in mind, he approached the bridge's communications console, where his superior, Lieutenant Paxton, was still compiling a report on message activity during his shift.

"You're early," Paxton said without looking up. "Of course, you're *always* early."

His tone, usually a good-natured one, sounded a trifle less so this morning. Ulelo chalked it up to the fact that Paxton wasn't used to working the graveyard shift—and wouldn't have done so this time either, except for the fact that one of the junior com officers had come down with a virus.

The transporter's biofilter strained out most alien parasites, but not all of them. Hence, the virus, which Greyhorse, the ship's chief medical officer, had been pleased to declare was "not much worse than a head cold."

Still, Paxton had been forced to replace the patient on her shift. Another com chief might have appointed someone else to do it, and gotten his usual hours of rest. But not Paxton. He never asked anyone to do something he wasn't willing to do himself.

Ulelo attempted to respond in a friendly, even playful way. "Are you complaining, sir?"

He wasn't by nature a playful person. However, he had come to realize that such banter was expected of him. It was expected of almost everyone on the ship, now that they had all gotten to know each other.

Paxton looked up at him and smiled a weary smile. "Not at all, Ulelo. Don't mind me. I'm a little . . . tired, I guess." With that, he finished what he was doing, got up, and moved aside.

Ulelo took the vacated seat and reviewed his superior's report. Nothing unusual, he noted as he went over it. Nothing that would pique anyone's interest.

That was fine with Ulelo. He didn't want anyone to have a reason to take a look at the com logs, so the more routine they were, the better.

"See you later," said Paxton. Then he headed for one of the aft consoles on some other bit of business, as he often did when his shift was over.

Ulelo waited a moment, until he was certain that Paxton wasn't coming back. As he sat there, he could hear the soft chirping of the other consoles, the even hum of the warp engines. He had gotten so accustomed to them, he hardly noticed them anymore.

Finally, the lieutenant took a quick look around to make certain no one was watching him. No one was, of course. No one *ever* watched him.

But then, why should they? Ulelo was an officer in good standing, a trusted member of the *Stargazer*'s crew. His record showed that his actions were beyond reproach.

That was why he had been given the responsibility of sending and receiving any number of subspace messages, some of them containing delicate and even classified information. But not the kind he was preparing to send now.

The transmission he was setting up at that particular moment contained strategic data on the *Stargazer*'s operating systems. Ulelo had gathered it painstakingly over the course of the last few days.

None of his superiors had asked him to either gather it or send it. In fact, they would have been shocked to know of his actions in this matter, which was why he was working in secret—just as he had done so many times before, over and over again, since the day he first set foot aboard the *Stargazer.*

After all, there was more to Dikembe Ulelo than met the eye.

On the surface, he was like anyone else on the ship. But inside, he was the minion of another set of masters, and it was on their behalf that he pursued his clandestine mission.

His preparations complete, Ulelo tapped in the command that would send out the packet of information. Then he returned the data to the file it had come from—a personal file, never seen by anyone else—and erased any evidence that it had ever been accessed from the communications console.

Done, he thought.

But before Ulelo could take any pride in the notion, he felt something strange—something he hadn't ever felt before on the bridge of the *Stargazer.*

Scrutiny.

Turning his head ever so slightly, he cast a glance in what he felt was the appropriate direction. It was then that he realized he was right. Someone was watching him, all right.

It was Lieutenant Paxton.

Why? Ulelo asked himself. Why was Paxton looking at him that way? What had he done to attract the man's attention?

Trying not to give anything away, Ulelo turned back to his console and forced himself to do some work—legitimate work, this time. But his heart was pounding so hard against his ribs that he thought they might break.

What is Paxton doing? he wondered, filled with a strange mixture of fear and curiosity. But he didn't dare glance in his superior's direction a second time.

Maybe he's not doing anything, Ulelo thought, and liked the sound of it. *Maybe he just happened to be looking at me for a moment. Maybe he still has no idea what I've been up to.*

Then he heard Paxton's voice, calm but firm: "Get up and step away from the console, Ulelo."

Ulelo turned to his superior again—he had to, having been addressed—and saw that Paxton was almost on top of him. He did his best to feign surprise: "Sir?"

"Step away from the console," Paxton repeated, a little more forcefully this time. His gaze was uncharacteristically hard and unyielding.

Ulelo's mind raced, seeking a way for him to wriggle off the hook. But he couldn't think of one.

Just then, the turbolift doors slid open and a couple of security officers stepped out. One was Joseph, the acting head of the section. The other was Pfeffer, one of the friends to whom Emily Bender had intoduced Ulelo.

Pfeffer's expression was unmistakably one of regret. Obviously, she knew what she had come for.

It was only then that Ulelo realized the extent to which he must have incriminated himself.

Paxton hadn't sent for the security officers. They had been waiting in the lift. So Paxton's suspicions weren't brand-new. He had known about Ulelo for some time.

A trap, Ulelo reflected.

"Come with us," said Joseph.

"Don't make it harder than it has to be," said Pfeffer, her eyes beseeching him to cooperate.

The other officers on the bridge had turned to them, wondering what in blazes was going on. Ulelo thought about protesting his innocence, stalling for some time.

But there was nothing to be gained by it. Without another word, he got up from his station and allowed his colleagues to escort him to the brig.

"Well," said Lieutenant Bender, as she set her tray down on the rectangular mess-hall table, "I hope I ordered the right thing, because I can't see worth a damn."

She had been studying alien microbes under a high-powered microviewer for the last several hours. If she hadn't officially gone blind, she had certainly come close enough.

Bender's friends at the table, Kochman and Vander-meer, glanced uncertainly at the food on her tray. Then they turned to each other, looks of grave concern on their faces.

"Should we tell her?" asked Kochman, one of the *Stargazer*'s junior navigation officers.

Vandermeer, a transporter operator, shrugged her shoulders. "Maybe she *likes* heart of *targ*."

"Heart of *targ . . . ?*" Bender echoed, pulling her chair out and depositing herself in its accommodating plastiform curve. What in blazes was *heart of* targ?

"A Klingon dish," Vandermeer explained. "Or so I've been told. I've never seen it myself."

"Until now, you mean," said Kochman, tilting his head meaningfully toward Bender's plate.

Vandermeer raised her hand to her mouth, obviously to conceal a smile. "Of course. Until *now.*"

"Actually," said Bender, happy to go along with the gag no matter *how* lame it was, "I've always been curious about Klingon cuisine. It's probably time I gave it a try."

And with that, she dug her fork into her pile of chicken cacciatore. Raising a piece of dusky meat covered with tomato tatters to the level of her eyes, she peered at it for a moment. Then she opened her mouth and slipped it inside.

"Mmm," she said, purposely speaking with her mouth full as she rounded up another forkful, "tastes just like chicken."

Bender had expected to get at least a chuckle from that, but none was forthcoming. Looking up, she saw that neither Kochman nor Vandermeer was even looking at her anymore. They were quite clearly looking *past* her.

The com officer cast a glance back over her shoulder to see what was more interesting than a mouthful of chicken cacciatore. What she saw was the advancing figure of Pug Joseph, the ship's acting security chief. Judging by the clouded expression on his face, Joseph hadn't come to the mess hall to satisfy a sweet tooth.

That was the first observation Bender made. The second, which came just a moment or two later, was that Joseph was headed precisely in her direction.

When he finally stopped in front of her, he didn't smile or greet her. He just said, "Lieutenant." And his tone was every bit as grim as his expression.

Joseph was acting downright ominous. And judging by the stares he was attracting from Bender's friends, she wasn't the only one who thought so.

"Is something wrong?" she asked.

Joseph didn't answer her question. All he told her was "I need you to come with me."

"What's going on?" Vandermeer asked.

The security chief didn't make any further reply. He just stood there, waiting for Bender to accompany him.

"Yes, sir," she said a little uncertainly.

Getting up from the table, she exchanged looks of

surprise with her companions. Then she did as Joseph had asked and followed him out of the mess hall.

Andreas Nikolas, formerly of the *Stargazer,* peered into the dense, twisted nest of finger-thick conduits glinting in the eerie beam of his palmlight.

"Obviously," he said, "this isn't the first time this power relay has been repaired."

His pal Eddie Locklear chuckled, his freckled face and unruly red hair thrown into sharp relief. It was Locklear who had gotten Nikolas a job on the cargo hauler *Iktoj'ni,* where he could put some of his Starfleet experience to work.

"I've personally dug into it at least a half-dozen times," Locklear told him, "and I only shipped out on this bucket a couple of years ago."

"Comforting," said Nikolas.

"Shut up and pass the hyperspanner," his friend told him.

Nikolas rummaged through the leathery bag of tools with his free hand. Finally, he came up with the one Locklear had asked for—a metallic, Y-shaped device designed to seal off old conduits and open new ones.

"Here you go," he said.

As Locklear took the device, he cast a grin at his friend. "I'll bet you never saw anything like these on those big, shiny Federation starships."

"Not once," Nikolas conceded.

He watched Locklear turn the hyperspanner on, a yellow-white energy field appearing between the tool's upper projections. Somehow, even that managed to look sickly and second-rate.

"This shouldn't take long," said Locklear.

"Meaning what?" asked Nikolas. "Twenty minutes?"

His friend didn't say. He just laughed, leaving the answer to Nikolas's imagination.

Clearly, the *Iktoj'ni* didn't have the state-of-the-art equipment found on the *Stargazer*. And judging by the tangled mess of conduit cables in the power relay, she didn't have the expertise one found on the *Stargazer* either.

Still, Nikolas was certain that he had made the right choice in putting Starfleet behind him. He saw that more clearly with every passing day.

On the *Iktoj'ni,* he didn't have to worry about seeing Gerda or Idun in the mess hall or some corridor. He wasn't constantly reminded of what he had lost when Gerda Idun vanished.

Of course, he missed his friends from time to time, his buddy Obal in particular. The Binderian had really grown on him in the short time they had served together.

But Nikolas didn't regret moving on. Not in the least. Or so he told himself.

Bender had never seen the inside of Captain Picard's ready room. She had only heard about it.

It was a good deal smaller than she had imagined, a good deal closer and more confining. Or maybe it was just her discomfort in being there that made it seem that way.

Technically, she wasn't alone. Pug Joseph was

keeping her company as she stood there. But for all the talking he was doing, she might as well have been alone for real.

"You've got to tell me *something*," she said at last.

The security chief looked sympathetic, but he didn't make an attempt to satisfy her curiosity. All he said was "The captain will be here soon."

Bender frowned. For the life of her, she couldn't figure out what was going on.

Suddenly, she saw the door slide open, yielding to a familiar figure—that of the captain. As Picard entered the room, he looked every bit as grim as Joseph did. Not a good sign. But at least Bender would find out why she was there.

"Lieutenant," said the captain, acknowledging her presence. He came around his desk, clearly in no great hurry, and sat down. "Thank you for coming."

I didn't know I had a choice in the matter, Bender thought. "Can you tell me why I'm here, sir?"

Picard nodded. "It's Lieutenant Ulelo."

Dikembe . . . ? "Is he all right?"

"His health is not the problem."

Bender didn't understand. "Then what *is?*"

"Apparently," said Picard, "Lieutenant Ulelo has been using his position as com officer to transmit technical data on the *Stargazer* to an unknown party."

He might as well have said that Ulelo was a Regulan bloodworm. It would have made as much sense.

"There must be some mistake," said Bender, her throat uncomfortably tight all of a sudden.

"I wish there was," the captain said, with what

seemed like utter sincerity. "Unfortunately, there is no question as to Ulelo's guilt in this matter. He was caught red-handed—in the act, as it were."

She couldn't believe it. *Wouldn't* believe it. Not from Ulelo. "Can I speak with him?"

"Not at this time," said Picard, "but soon enough."

It wasn't what Bender had hoped to hear. "If I could see him," she asked, "get his side of the story . . ."

The captain frowned a little, but remained unmoved. "Clearly," he said, "this comes as a shock to you. I expected no less. However, you are Ulelo's closest friend on the *Stargazer,* and—as you can imagine—it is important to us to identify the recipient of his transmissions."

There is no recipient, Bender insisted inwardly. It didn't matter what anyone said. Ulelo couldn't have done it.

Unaware of her thoughts, Picard went on. "Do you recall his having said anything, at any time, that might shed some light on this matter for us?"

She shook her head—too soon to give the captain the impression that she had fairly considered his question. But he didn't take her to task for it.

He simply said, "Perhaps later, when you have had some time to think about it. Dismissed, Lieutenant."

Bender was about to ask again to see her friend, but she could tell it wouldn't do any good. Feeling numb and a bit unreal, she left Picard's ready room and—abandoning the idea of eating anything—wandered in the direction of her quarters.

Chapter Five

WU GAZED AT LIEUTENANT ULELO across the yellowish shimmer of the electromagnetic barrier that incarcerated him. He was sitting on the bed provided for his use, looking up at her.

If Wu had expected Ulelo to look repentant, he wasn't. He didn't even look worried, though he had to know that he was headed for a Federation penal colony.

But he didn't look arrogant either. More than anything, he reminded the second officer of a small boy, caught up in something he didn't quite understand.

A small boy, Wu reminded herself, who had put one over on all of them, betraying his crewmates and sending information on any number of key operating systems to some mysterious third party.

She glanced at Pierzynski, the security officer on duty, and nodded. In response, Pierzynski fingered a code into the touch-sensitive, metal-alloy plate set into the bulkhead next to Ulelo's cell.

A moment later, the barrier was gone. Wu stepped inside the enclosure, which housed a chair in addition to the prisoner's bed, and then glanced at Pierzynski again. Inputting another code, the security officer restored the barrier.

Wu sat down in the chair and waited a moment. She wanted to see if Ulelo had anything to say for himself—protests of innocence, that sort of thing.

He didn't. He just looked at her.

"Well," she said finally, in an attempt to loosen things up, "to tell you the truth, I never pictured us having a conversation here in the brig."

Ulelo frowned a little, but didn't say anything in response.

It was all right. Wu hadn't expected him to confess right off the bat. Not after he had run a covert operation for months without so much as a bead of sweat.

"I'd like you to answer some questions," she said. "If you cooperate, it may make a difference in your sentence."

He remained silent.

Wu saw that she had her work cut out for her.

"Our logs indicate a series of transmissions over the last several weeks. You made those transmissions, yes?"

Ulelo nodded.

At least he's not denying it. "Each transmission," said the second officer, "contained technical specs on one or more of the *Stargazer*'s systems. This was information you initially collected in your personal files."

Again, the prisoner nodded.

"And when you had enough to justify the risk, you sent it—right from your com station."

Another nod. Wu was encouraged.

"What I find puzzling," she said, "is that those transmissions weren't sent to any set of coordinates twice. They were sent in what seems like every possible direction."

Ulelo had no comment.

"What were you trying to accomplish?" she asked.

"I was following orders," he said, surprising her.

Now we're getting somewhere. "*Whose* orders?"

Ulelo fell silent again.

But Wu wasn't going to give up so easily. "Lieutenant, you said you were following orders. I asked you whose they were."

The com officer just stared at her.

"Was it the Ubarrak?" she ventured, groping in the dark.

He shook his head. "No."

Good, Wu thought. *If we can't get a direct answer, maybe we can at least narrow it down.*

"The Cardassians?"

Ulelo hesitated this time. But in the end, he answered in the negative again.

Wu searched his eyes. Did his hesitation mean something? Was it the Cardassians after all?

She didn't let on about her suspicion. Why put the com officer on his guard? Maybe he would say something later that would nail it down for her.

"The Klingons?" she asked.

The Federation wasn't at odds with the Empire these days. Still, one never knew. . . .

"No," said Ulelo, as easily as he had ruled out the Ubarrak. No hesitation at all that time.

There weren't too many other possibilities. Of course, Ulelo could have been in cahoots with a party heretofore undiscovered by the Federation, but Wu couldn't inquire about entities of which she was unaware.

Ulelo would have to volunteer that kind of information. And judging from the way their conversation was going, he wasn't about to do that.

"What about the Aristaani?" she suggested.

It was a belligerent species, and one with which the Federation had butted heads on occasion. But to Wu's knowledge, they weren't the type to engage in espionage.

That made it all the more surprising when Ulelo said, "Yes."

He said it freely, too—as if he had no compunctions about saying it. And yet he hadn't been willing to mention the Aristaani when Wu had asked him an open-ended question.

She didn't understand. Unless Ulelo was trying to deceive her, throw her off the trail . . .

But her instincts, and the look on his face, told her that he wasn't doing that at all. He was telling her the truth. She would have bet on it.

"The Aristaani," she said, just to be sure.

Ulelo nodded. "Yes."

But the more she thought about it, the less she believed it. The Aristaani were even more bullheaded and battle-hungry than the Klingons. It had always been their practice to meet their enemies head-on.

So why change now? Wu wished she knew.

"Did the Aristaani tell you what they were planning to do with this information?"

Ulelo shook his head. "No."

Of course not. That would have made Wu's job too easy. "How did you come to work for them?"

The prisoner's eyes seemed to glaze over for a moment. Then he said, "Work for whom?"

What is this, a game? "The Aristaani."

A strange look came over Ulelo's face. An almost frightened look. "I didn't work for the Aristaani."

"You just said you *did,*" Wu told him, feeling more than a hint of annoyance now.

The prisoner shook his head from side to side. "No," he said, "not the Aristaani. The *Andorians.*"

"The Andorians . . . ?" she echoed incredulously.

The Andorians were members of the Federation. Some of their people were serving on Federation starships. It seemed unlikely that they would go to such trouble to obtain technical information on the *Stargazer.*

Ulelo looked at her, his eyes full of innocence. "Yes."

Anger tightened Wu's jaw. "Do you know what you're saying, Lieutenant?"

His eyes glazed over again, as if he were trying to see something far away. "No," he whispered, "not the Andorians. Of course not. It was the Vulcans. . . ."

Wu took a breath, then let it out. *The Vulcans.* As if that made any sense at all.

It was pretty clear that she wasn't going to get anything out of Ulelo. What *wasn't* clear was *why*. Was he just pretending to have lost his mind in order to stonewall her? Or was there something truly wrong with him?

One thing was certain: She wasn't going to find out by remaining in the brig. Getting to her feet, she signaled to Pierzynski, who had been watching from the other side of the barrier.

The security officer let Wu out, then reactivated the forcefield. It hummed a little—or rather, its generators did—as the second officer paused to consider Ulelo again.

He looked peaceful once more, innocent, returning her scrutiny with the same mild interest he had shown earlier. It was as if they hadn't had a conversation at all.

Wu regarded him a moment longer. Then she looked up at the intercom grid hidden in the ceiling and said, "Wu to Doctor Greyhorse."

"This is Greyhorse," came the reply.

"I'd like you to examine Ulelo," Wu told him.

"You think there's something wrong with him?" Greyhorse asked. He sounded skeptical.

"I'm not sure," she said. "He seems confused at times. Muddled. Hardly the behavior of a man clever enough to do the things we've accused him of doing. I want to find out why."

"All right," said the doctor. "Bring him down to sickbay. I'll put him through the ringer."

"Thank you," said the second officer. "Wu out."

* * *

"It angers me," said Gerda Asmund.

Her twin sister, Idun, who was sitting beside her at the *Stargazer's* helm console, glanced at Gerda. "Ulelo?"

"Yes," said Gerda, the muscles bunching in her jaw. "Ulelo." She said the name as if it were rancid meat, as if she found each syllable more loathsome than the one before it.

Idun was angry as well. As someone who had been raised on Klingon virtues, she despised the notion of treachery. It made her skin crawl like a plate of serpent worms.

She remembered the stories her Klingon father had told them about those who betrayed kin and comrades. There was Lifdag, who—appalled by his brother Farrl's treachery—not only killed Farrl but took his own life thereafter. And then there was Tupran, son of Tuprox, who opened the doors of his father's house to its enemies—and ironically became their first victim.

Traitors were even worse than cowards, Idun's father had said. Tradition said that cowards were to be shunned, but traitors had to be killed on sight.

Gerda made a sound of disgust. "Had I been the first to discover Ulelo's deceit, I might not have been as patient or as restrained as Lieutenant Paxton."

Idun felt the same way. Once Ulelo's guilt became plain to her, it would have been difficult indeed not to go after him.

"But you *didn't* know," she reminded her sister. "You never even suspected that Ulelo had another agenda." Which was why Gerda and Idun were as surprised as anyone when security showed up and took the com officer away.

"You're right," said Gerda, her voice husky with emotion. "I didn't suspect Ulelo. I didn't question his loyalty for a moment." She turned to Idun, her eyes hard and fierce. "And *that* is precisely what angers me."

There were three of them in the captain's ready room—Wu, Greyhorse, and Picard himself.

The doctor, who didn't come to see the captain there very often—didn't leave his office very often, for that matter—looked cramped and constrained. It wasn't just that the plastiform chair was too small to accommodate his bulk. It seemed that the whole room was too small for him.

"You have examined Ulelo," said Picard, already regretting that he hadn't called this meeting in the roomier precincts of Greyhorse's sickbay.

"I have indeed," said the medical officer. "Actually, I gave Ulelo a routine checkup just the other day and found nothing of concern. But at Commander Wu's request, I ran an expanded battery of tests on him—including anything I could think of that seemed at all relevant to Ulelo's situation."

"And?" the captain asked.

"By all physical standards," said the chief medical officer, "Ulelo is the picture of health. No chemical imbalances, no blockages, no evidence of injury. In short, nothing that would result in aberrational behavior."

Picard shifted in his seat. "Then—"

Greyhorse held up a peremptory hand, disregarding

the difference in their ranks. "I also conducted a test that wasn't strictly medical. I asked Ulelo some yes-or-no questions—and monitored his nervous system when he answered."

"A lie-detector test," Wu noted.

"Precisely," said Greyhorse. "I began by asking Ulelo about the Klingons, since they came up in the course of your conversation with him. Without hesitation, he identified the Klingons as our enemies. And yet, when I asked him about the Klingons a few minutes later, he said just as unhesitatingly that they were our allies."

The doctor turned to Picard. "Like Commander Wu, I found myself wondering if Ulelo was up to something. But his readouts showed that he wasn't lying. At the time he made those statements, *he actually believed them.*"

"So his problem is a psychological one," Picard concluded.

"Evidently," said Greyhorse. "The funny thing is that Ulelo is absolutely lucid in most respects, especially those that pertain to his work as a communications officer. But when it comes to other parts of his life, he seems lost."

He shrugged his mountainous shoulders. "I wasn't trained to be a counselor. However, I would say Ulelo is schizophrenic—out of touch with certain aspects of our reality."

The captain looked at him, taking a moment to absorb the implications, which were considerable. "If that is so, then his periodic data transmissions . . . ?"

"Were harmless," said the medical officer. "Exercises in fantasy, sent to no one. Or rather, no one who exists outside the precincts of Ulelo's mind."

"Harmless," Picard repeated.

"If you ask me," said Greyhorse, "yes."

Picard nodded. "Thank you, Doctor." He turned to Wu. "I will make arrangements to get the lieutenant to an appropriate facility for more complete diagnosis and treatment. But while he is on the *Stargazer,* I would like him kept in the brig—just in case."

Wu agreed that that would be the wisest course of action, Greyhorse's observations notwithstanding. Then the captain adjourned the meeting.

After Picard watched his officers depart, Greyhorse more eagerly than Wu, he sat in his desk chair for a moment. *After all that,* he told himself.

For Ulelo's treachery to be identified as a symptom of a damaged psyche . . . it was shocking. Almost as shocking, in fact, as finding out about the lieutenant's transgression in the first place.

And yet, it was rather a relief, wasn't it? They would all breathe easier knowing that Ulelo's confederates were waking dreams, and nothing more.

Ensign Jiterica surveyed her new appearance in the mirror that hung from her closet door.

Until now, she hadn't made much use of either the closet or the reflective surface. But then, her only garment had been her containment suit, one specially retrofitted with her unusual set of needs in mind.

Jiterica's species, the Nizhrak'a, had evolved in the atmosphere of a gas giant in the Sonada Sin system.

Had she still been there, she could have expanded to her full volume and flowed naturally from wind to fierce, ragged wind. But on a starship, made for beings much more dense and compact than herself, she had to operate in a severely condensed form.

Hence, the stiff, bulky suit that Jiterica had endured almost every moment of every day. It had been perhaps the most difficult part of her adjustment to life on the *Stargazer,* and that was saying something.

But she hadn't imagined that she had any alternative. She could either wear the suit or surrender any hope of functioning as an officer in Starfleet.

Until now.

The suit Jiterica had just put on was considerably more streamlined and lightweight than the other one, and considerably easier to manipulate. It made her look more like the other crewmen on board—the female crewmen in particular.

"What do you think?" asked Simenon, who was standing behind her in his lab coat, his arms folded across his chest.

"It's . . . wonderful," she said.

Before, the Nizhrak's artificial voice had been tinny, unnatural. Even she had been able to hear that after a while. Now the speech sounds she made were virtually indistinguishable from those made by humanoid throats.

"Good," said Simenon, who had designed and manufactured the new suit with the help of a replicator. "And I take it the forcefield is doing its job?"

"Perfectly," she told him. Or at least, as well as the forcefield in her other suit.

"Try sitting," he said.

Jiterica moved to her bed and sat down. It was a considerably less arduous task than it had been before. But then, her suit was nearly as flexible as living epidermis—or so Simenon had assured her.

She looked at herself in the mirror again. It might have been one of the Asmunds sitting there in the suit, or Urajel, or Commander Wu. That's how well proportioned and at ease she looked.

Paris would be pleased when he returned.

But he would also be disturbed, as Jiterica was, by the situation surrounding Lieutenant Ulelo. News about him had spread through the *Stargazer* like a ripple of ionic wind on her homeworld, tearing at the bonds of trust and community that had been forged on the ship, making chaos of calm.

Fortunately, Ulelo's actions had been identified as the product of an unbalanced mind, attempts to connect to someone or something that never existed. The *Stargazer* wasn't in any danger.

However, it bothered Jiterica that Ulelo was something other than what he had seemed. Among her people, there was no such thing as subterfuge or deception, no possibility of treachery or betrayal.

Obviously, she reflected, *I still have a lot to learn about humanoids.*

Picard was standing by the single observation port in his ready room, taking in the beauty of the stars that were rushing past, when his weapons officer paid him an unexpected visit.

"Mister Vigo," he said, as the Pandrilite's impressive form was revealed on the threshold.

"Sir," said Vigo.

Normally he was a cheerful soul, his spirits remarkably difficult to dampen. But not at the moment. His face was as stern as Picard had ever seen it.

"You appear to have something on your mind," the captain observed.

"I didn't want to disturb you," he said, "while you were dealing with Lieutenant Ulelo, and the implications of what he had done. But now that we know he's harmless . . ."

"Yes?" said Picard.

Vigo's nostrils flared. "I've been thinking," he said. "About Ejanix. About the things he did . . . and said."

Ejanix had been a Pandrilite, like Vigo. In fact, he had been Vigo's mentor back on their homeworld.

In those days, Ejanix was known as a brilliant theoretician—brilliant enough to be invited to teach at Starfleet Academy, where he continued to distinguish himself. But his crowning achievements were to come on Wayland Prime, where Starfleet had established a think tank for weapons development.

His particular focus was on phaser technology—improving its range, its accuracy, its energy efficiency. It had seemed he was making progress on Wayland Prime, turning in the caliber of work everyone expected of him.

But he betrayed Starfleet and his colleagues by opening the installation to a band of Pandrilite terrorists, intending to help finance a revolution by selling

Starfleet's weapons research. And he would have succeeded had it not been for Vigo.

Eventually, Ejanix saw the error of his ways, and died heroically at the hands of his rebel allies. But that didn't erase the fact of his treachery—not in Picard's mind, and certainly not when it came to the official record.

"Go on," said the captain.

Vigo's gaze hardened. "I don't condone his treachery, you understand. Not for a minute."

The weapons officer fell into silence then. But Picard didn't make a move to fill it. Clearly, Vigo had more to say.

"And yet," he continued at last, "I feel it's a mistake to dismiss what he told me about Pandril."

The captain was intrigued. "And what, exactly, did he tell you about Pandril?"

Vigo heaved a sigh—an extravagant gesture, given his massive size and physique. "He said that Pandrilite society is out of balance—that the Lesser Castes are oppressed by the Elevated Castes, to which my family belongs. And that our governing council, when presented with evidence of this imbalance, looks the other way."

Picard hadn't heard any of this before. Obviously, Vigo had been keeping it to himself—and letting it fester like an untreated wound. "Is that why Ejanix decided to betray Starfleet?"

"Yes," said Vigo. "He felt there was no way within the system to obtain justice for the Lesser Castes."

"However," the captain noted, "that may only have

been Ejanix's perception. The truth may be a different matter entirely."

The lieutenant looked contemplative for a moment. "Ejanix told me that I had been away from Pandril for too long, or I would have seen the Lesser Castes' oppression for myself. He suggested that I rectify the oversight."

Picard wasn't happy to hear that. "Rectify it how?" he asked. "By giving up your position on the *Stargazer* and returning to Pandril? What are we talking about?"

"A leave of absence." Vigo looked at his superior beseechingly. "An *indefinite* leave of absence."

"I see," said the captain. He leaned back in his chair to ponder the idea. "And what if you find that the situation on Pandril is as Ejanix said?"

"Then those in the upper castes should be made aware of it—preferably by a member of their own caste. And if I must be the one to tell them, I accept that responsibility."

Picard frowned. It was clear that Vigo had given the matter a good deal of thought, and that his decision hadn't been an easy one.

He didn't like the idea of losing his senior weapons officer—especially when the sector was so unsettled. However, if anyone had earned his understanding, it was Vigo.

"I will grant you such a leave," the captain said, "if that is what you really want."

"It is," said Vigo. "But," he was quick to add, "I don't want to leave you understaffed."

Picard smiled. "It is not as if I will not miss your

expertise, Lieutenant. However, we *do* have other experienced weapons officers. I am certain that we will get by, if returning to Pandril is that important to you."

Vigo nodded. "Thank you, sir."

"You are welcome," said Picard.

He had long ago made it a policy never to stand in the way of his crew. If Vigo had a personal mission to carry out, the captain would do everything in his power to facilitate it.

He just hoped he wouldn't have occasion to regret it.

Ben Zoma had been counting the hours until his shuttle got within transporter range of the *Antares* and he could say good-bye to the erstwhile Arlen McAteer.

The first officer had met men inclined toward criticism before, but he had never met anyone inclined toward so *much* criticism. It seemed that whatever minute detail Ben Zoma or his security officers took care of, there was a better way to handle it—and McAteer was generous enough to share it with them.

Ben Zoma had a hard time believing it was completely a matter of duty. It seemed to him that McAteer was practicing for the moment when he would put Picard in front of a competency hearing—a proceeding in which the admiral would not only present the case for Picard's demotion, but also rule on it.

But that was the way of it in such hearings. Expediency ruled. If justice was served, it was strictly a coincidence.

Ben Zoma glanced for what might have been the

thousandth time at the chronometer set into the shuttle's helm console. One hour and ten minutes until they could drop off McAteer and head for home.

Normally, he wouldn't have been in any hurry to contact their rendezvous partner. But in this case, he couldn't wait. "Hail the *Antares,*" he told Garner, who was now riding shotgun.

"Aye, sir," she said.

The admiral turned to Ramirez, the lovely, dark-haired security officer who had wound up next to him, and said, "Too bad you won't have the opportunity to spend some time with Captain Vayishra. I think you'd learn a few things."

Feeling the sting of implied criticism, Ben Zoma leaned forward from his seat in the rear. "I've learned quite a bit from Captain Picard, sir."

McAteer cast a steely glance in Ben Zoma's direction. "I'm sure you have, Commander."

But the admiral wasn't saying whether what Ben Zoma had learned was good or bad. His teeth grinding together, the first officer toyed with the notion of a response—until he saw the expression of surprise on Garner's face.

"What's the matter?" he asked.

Garner turned to look back at him. "I'm afraid there's no answer, sir."

"No answer?" McAteer echoed. "Are you sure, Lieutenant?"

Garner nodded. "I am, sir."

Ben Zoma frowned. The *Antares* should have been well within communications range by now. If she wasn't, there was no way she was going to make the rendezvous in time.

Of course, starships experienced communications glitches from time to time—and for all kinds of reasons, ranging from the mechanical to the celestial. Sometimes the problem was as simple as a crossed circuit.

It was inconvenient, but it happened. *No reason to be concerned,* Ben Zoma reflected.

"Keep trying," he told Garner.

The lieutenant assured him that she would do that.

Chapter Six

THOUGH CAPTAIN DENTON GREENBRIAR sat in front of the seemingly infinite river of suns displayed on his bridge's forward viewscreen, his mind was on none of them.

Or rather, it was on a sun not yet shown on the screen—the one that warmed the fertile, mineral-rich world known as Mizar II. Thanks to their ample resources, the Mizarians had been assaulted by one species after the other over the last few hundred years. On two occasions, it had been the Ubarrak. And yet the Mizarians had never made the slightest move to defend themselves, much less to seek assistance from others.

From time to time, the Federation had offered to intervene. But the Mizarians had always sent them away. They seemed to believe that as bad as the situation was for them, any demonstration of backbone would only invite something worse.

The Federation hadn't always been good at taking a hint. But eventually, it stopped offering.

Then, just a couple of weeks ago, the Federation Council had received a surprise communication from Mizar II—or more specifically, from a new government that seemed to have more gumption than its predecessors. For the first time, the Mizarians were making inquiries about Federation membership.

Someone would have to ferry an ambassador to Mizar II to answer the Mizarians' questions. The job pulled Greenbriar and his ship, the *Cochise,* off the Ubarrak border, where they had been stationed for the last several months.

At the moment, the ambassador in question—a gray-haired Vulcan by the name of Surat—was meditating in his quarters, having left instructions for Greenbriar to rouse him when the *Cochise* dropped out of warp. But that wouldn't happen for a few more hours, so Surat would be *very* much at peace when he arrived.

The captain settled back in his seat. He didn't particularly like this part of his job—moving dignitaries around the Federation—but he had long ago accepted it.

Besides, with politics in the sector coming to a boil, he and his crew would be called on to fight before too long. It was inevitable. The time would come when he would look back fondly on moments like these, and wish he had enjoyed them while he had the chance.

Greenbriar turned to his helm officer, Hohauser. "How are we doing, Lieutenant?"

Other ships had detected subspace anomalies in this part of space, so they had taken the *Cochise* around them. But dealing with such phenomena was an imprecise business at best.

"So far, so good," reported Hohauser from his place behind the helm console.

The captain considered asking for more information, but decided against it. Hohauser was an old hand at this, having served under Greenbriar even before they launched the *Cochise*. His other bridge officers were veterans as well. If they thought he needed to know something, they would tell him.

That was the secret of his reputation as a model captain. He surrounded himself with the right people and did his best not to get in their way.

Just as Greenbriar thought that, he saw Cangelosi—his navigation officer—tuck a lock of hair behind her ear. He knew what that meant. She did it whenever she had come across something unexpected.

The captain leaned forward. "What is it?"

"I've got something on sensors," said Cangelosi, a slender, dark-haired woman. She manipulated her controls. "It's a vessel, sir."

"On screen," said Greenbriar.

A moment later, he got a chance to see the ship in question. It was a short, thick cylinder with two wide, flat pieces projecting from either side of it. The captain had never seen anything even remotely like it.

"Any idea whose that is?" he asked Hohauser.

"There's no match in our files, sir."

Greenbriar considered the vessel. Then he turned to Moy, his com officer. "Hail her, Lieutenant."

"Aye, sir," said Moy, bending to the task with characteristic alacrity. But a moment later, he looked up. "No response."

"She just changed course," Cangelosi reported. She glanced at the captain. "She's heading right for us, sir."

Greenbriar absorbed the information. *Now,* he asked himself, *why would an unidentified vessel in Federation space refuse to answer hails and then adopt an intercept course?* Why indeed . . . unless she was spoiling for a fight?

His instincts told him that he would be trading torpedo volleys before he knew it—even if he didn't have the slightest idea why. Then again, not every species in the universe adhered to the idea that violence required an explanation. Some of them just showed up with their weapon ports firing.

Of course, there was always the possibility that Greenbriar would find a way to defuse the situation. That was his preference, as always. But in case he couldn't handle the encounter peacefully, he wanted to be prepared for the alternative.

"Red alert," he said, and watched his bridge take on a crimson hue. "Shields up. Power weapons." He turned to Moy again. "Keep trying to establish contact."

"Aye, sir," said the com officer.

"Distance?" Greenbriar asked.

"Ten billion kilometers and closing," said Cangelosi.

A minute and a half, the captain thought. That was

all the time they had to figure this out. Then the mystery vessel would be in range of the Starfleet ship's photon torpedoes—and more than likely, vice versa.

"Still no response," said Moy.

The strange vessel was looming larger and larger on the viewscreen. Greenbriar frowned. His first officer had gone to sleep only a couple of hours earlier, but he would want to know what was going on.

Looking up at the intercom grid, the captain said, "Commander Dolgin, wake up. You there, Alex?"

A moment passed. "Dolgin here," came a tired voice.

Greenbriar described the situation as concisely as possible. "I thought you'd like to know."

"On my way," snapped the first officer.

"Five billion kilometers," said Cangelosi.

Next, Greenbriar interrupted the ambassador's meditation. Diplomatic types often got in the way at times like these, but all Surat did was acknowledge the captain's warning.

Vulcans, Greenbriar mused. *You've got to love them.*

Just then, the turbolift doors hissed open and his first officer emerged. Alexander Dolgin was a short, wiry man with a receding hairline and a head for starship operations. As he advanced to the captain's chair, Greenbriar said, "That was record time."

"Imagine if I hadn't stopped to take a shower," said the first officer.

"Two billion kilometers," said Cangelosi.

Moy sighed with frustration. "Still nothing, sir."

That was it, then. Those in the mystery vessel were

determined to start a fight, and Greenbriar and his crew had no choice but to defend themselves.

Fortunately, they had gone toe-to-toe with marauders many times before, and they had always come out on top. The captain had every confidence that they would do so this time as well.

"Range," said Bolaris, his Andorian tactical officer.

"Their weapons are charged," Cangelosi noted.

"Stand by," said Greenbriar.

Despite appearances, there was a chance the mystery vessel was just trying to intimidate them. That happened sometimes. So the captain would give his adversary a free shot, if that was what it came to. He wouldn't authorize a volley until his adversary released one first.

Greenbriar took a breath and let it out slowly. *Come on. Don't make me rip you apart. Show some sense.*

And for a moment, it looked like the mystery vessel might do that. Then Bolaris yelled out, "She's firing!"

Suddenly, a mess of pale green beams erupted at them, coming from half a dozen recessed weapons ports. It was an impressive-looking barrage—the type of firepower the *Cochise* herself might have displayed if Greenbriar had been intent on turning an enemy into space dust.

"Evasive maneuvers!" he called out.

Hohauser reacted as brilliantly as ever, getting every last bit of speed and maneuverability out of the *Cochise*. He couldn't escape the mystery ship's beams entirely, but at worst they would take a glancing blow.

Or so it seemed to Greenbriar—until he felt a violent shudder run through the ship, as if she had been slapped by a giant hand.

What was that? he wondered, hanging on to his armrests. The way Hohauser had slipped the brunt of the attack, they should barely have felt a thing.

"Sir," said Cangelosi, a strain of puzzlement in her voice, "shields are down eighteen percent."

Greenbriar was puzzled as well. He got up to confirm Cangelosi's reading and saw that she was right. Eighteen percent—when they had barely been grazed? It didn't seem possible.

Judging by the look on Dolgin's face, he didn't think so either. And Dolgin wasn't an easy man to impress.

"Return fire!" Greenbriar commanded, and the *Cochise* unleashed a directed-energy barrage of her own.

It struck the alien vessel amidships, delivering an impact that should have made her commander think twice about continuing the fray. But the enemy didn't seem daunted in the least. In fact, she came after the *Cochise* a second time, her weapons ports blazing with redoubled fury.

This time, the captain didn't have to call for evasive action. His helm officer was already on it, wrenching them hard to port.

Again, the enemy's beams barely grazed them. And again, Greenbriar felt his ship shudder as if it had been pounded.

What's going on here? he asked himself. Then, because he couldn't come up with an answer, he posed the same question out loud.

But no one else had an answer either—not even Dolgin, who was known to have an answer for *everything*. And before they could give the matter any real thought, the enemy placed the *Cochise* in her sights again.

This time, Hohauser wasn't able to give them the slip. When the energy barrage hit, it jerked the deck out from under Greenbriar's feet, sending him staggering into a bulkhead.

Thrusting himself off it, he saw one of the aft consoles explode. Fortunately, his science officer was no longer sitting in front of it, since she had been slammed to the deck.

A cloud of sparks and black smoke rose from the console, drawing the attention of a crewman with a fire extinguisher. But the bridge was already filling with the smell of burning conduits.

"Shields down seventy-eight percent!" Cangelosi barked. "Hull breaches on decks eight and nine!"

Greenbriar muttered a curse. In the past, his deflectors had held up under worse punishment. What made the aliens' fire so damned effective against them?

"Casualties?" Dolgin asked.

"Coming in now, sir," said Moy. "Crewmen down on decks eight, nine, and ten. Medical teams are on their way."

Greenbriar watched the enemy ship on his viewscreen. She was dogging them but holding her fire—as if she knew she could take out the *Cochise* whenever she wanted.

The captain was determined to show the aliens the

pitfalls of overconfidence. "Give me a full torpedo spread," he ordered his weapons officer.

"Aye, sir," came Bolaris's reply, his antennae twitching. And a moment later: "Ready when you are, sir."

Greenbriar didn't hesitate. "Fire!"

The *Cochise*'s torpedo launchers sent their matter-antimatter payloads streaking across the void like a swarm of golden arrows. And Bolaris's aim was perfect. The missiles struck the enemy dead-on, the spectacle of their impact causing Greenbriar to lose sight of his adversary for a moment.

That'll teach them, he thought, and returned to his chair.

But when the light display faded and the enemy was visible again, it was obvious that she was still intact. No—better than that, Greenbriar mused bitterly. She hadn't even been scratched by the torpedo barrage.

The captain wasn't often given to profanity, but he swore under his breath a second time. This was insane. It reminded him of a nightmare he had had once, where he was fighting a boyhood adversary but none of his blows had any effect.

But why should that be? What made this vessel different from any of the others Greenbriar had encountered over the years? What was her secret?

He would have dearly loved to know the answer to that question. But the way this battle was going, he didn't dare allow the *Cochise* to linger a moment longer.

"Get us out of here," he told Hohauser.

The helmsman wasn't used to hearing those words

from Greenbriar, but he took them in stride and brought the *Cochise* about. Then he accelerated to warp eight.

However, the mystery vessel didn't seem willing to let them off the hook. She came about and matched the starship's speed, remaining in weapons range.

The captain eyed the viewscreen, which showed him a rear view now. His adversary seemed content to keep pace for the time being, but he didn't expect that situation to prevail much longer.

"Full power to rear deflectors," he said, anticipating the worst. And a moment later, he got it.

The barrage that blossomed from the enemy's weapons ports was as beautiful as anything Greenbriar had ever seen. The screen filled with its splendor.

The captain braced himself against the impact, but it didn't help. He was shot out of his chair as if by a catapult. Somehow, he managed to avoid hitting anything except the deck, but even that was enough to stun him for a moment.

As he regained his senses, he looked around—and saw Dolgin stretched out on the deck. *Dead?* the captain wondered disbelievingly, as he moved to the commander's side. *Or maybe just unconscious?* He couldn't tell—until Dolgin stirred, sending a stab of relief through his superior.

But Dolgin wasn't the only one who had been injured by the blast. Cangelosi was cradling what looked like a broken arm as she tried to crawl back behind her console, and a stunned Moy was bleeding from a gash over his eye.

All around them, the bridge was a vision of hell, a

roiling, spark-shot chaos. Consoles were aflame. The air was thick with smoke and getting thicker. And alarms were going off as if the ship herself were screaming in terror.

But as Greenbriar dragged himself to his feet, he saw that at least a couple of his officers were still at their stations. Hohauser was still bent over his helm console, trying desperately to outmaneuver the enemy, and Bolaris was still poking at his weapons controls.

"Fire at will!" the captain told Bolaris, his voice a smoke-parched croak.

The weapons officer shook his head, disappointment etched into his face. "I can't, sir. They've disabled our weapons ports—phasers as well as torpedoes."

"Shields are down too," rasped Cangelosi. She was in the process of moving back behind her console, broken arm and all. "We won't be able to take another barrage."

Greenbriar's jaw clenched. He just wished he knew what the aliens were after. He could reason with them then, maybe save some lives. But he was still in the dark.

"Captain," said Cangelosi, looking up at him with smoke-stung eyes full of horror, "they're beaming aboard!"

"Where?" asked Greenbriar.

"Decks five and six," said the navigator.

Five and six? But there was nothing there except crew quarters. Obviously, the intruders' sensors weren't nearly as advanced as their tactical systems.

The captain understood Cangelosi's reaction to the enemy's presence aboard the *Cochise*. It was a natural enough response for someone who plied the void of space, and felt only as secure as the metal-alloy shell around her. But far from being horrified, Greenbriar was encouraged.

The aliens wouldn't have beamed over if they meant to destroy the ship. That just stood to reason. So for a while, at least, the *Cochise* would be safe from another barrage.

All the captain would have to worry about were the boarding parties. But he felt confident that his crew could hold them off, there on their home turf.

Let them come, he thought. *We'll take our chances.*

Looking up at the intercom, Greenbriar briefed his crew as to the problem. "All hands," he said, "break out phasers. Take any measures necessary to defend yourselves and your ship."

Fortunately, there was a phaser locker there on the bridge. Before the captain had finished advising the crew, Bolaris had opened the locker and begun distributing its contents.

By then also, a medical team had arrived to see to Dolgin and the others. But Greenbriar didn't have the luxury of helping them pack his exec on a gurney. He had to get hold of a phaser and get himself down to deck five.

If his people were battling the invaders down there, he wanted to battle alongside them.

Paris sighed.

"Don't worry," said a voice, just loud enough to be heard. "She'll still be there when you get back."

The ensign turned to Ben Zoma, who was sitting

beside him with a knowing smile on his face. Paris felt a hot rush of blood in his cheeks. How could the first officer have known that he was thinking about Jiterica?

"Sir . . . ?" he said, not knowing what else to say.

Ben Zoma chuckled. "I'd know that sigh anywhere, Mister Paris. It's an 'I miss my girl' sigh, an 'I wonder what she's doing right now' sigh. Believe me, I've been there."

The ensign looked back at the others. Chen, Horombo, and Ramirez were leaning back in their seats with their eyes closed—maybe asleep, maybe not. McAteer and Garner were going over a schematic in the rear of the craft, one of many the admiral had asked to see over the last few hours.

As far as Paris could tell, none of them was eavesdropping on Ben Zoma. The ensign was relieved.

Not that his feelings for Jiterica were any big secret, really. It was just that he had never had occasion to discuss them with anyone.

No, Paris thought, *there's more to it than that.* He was concerned about how people would react. Jiterica was, after all, a low-density being, vastly different from anyone he had ever met. Once their relationship became common knowledge, it was bound to raise a few eyebrows.

"Relax," said Ben Zoma. "I wouldn't have said anything if I thought anyone was listening."

Paris felt comfortable with the first officer. Everyone did. But he still didn't feel right discussing Jiterica.

"I *was* thinking about someone" was all he cared to admit.

The first officer nodded. "That's what happens on these long away missions. Every minute seems like an hour, especially when you're not going anywhere."

True, thought Paris.

"And that person you're used to seeing every day, several times a day, isn't with you. Suddenly, it feels like she never was, and never will be again. But you'll see her again, Ensign. Believe me."

Paris relaxed enough to smile back. "I do, sir."

When Greenbriar arrived on deck five, two of his people were sprawled motionless on the deck already, and two more had their backs plastered against the bulkhead with their weapons extended.

But there was no sign of the invaders.

Bolting across the corridor, he joined the two defenders. One was O'Connor, a pretty blond science officer. The other was Sasaki, a stocky, bald-headed engineer.

"How many?" Greenbriar breathed into O'Connor's ear.

"Hard to tell," she said. "Five, maybe six. We haven't seen them for a minute or so, but they're still there."

"Did you get any of them?" he asked.

"Two," said O'Connor. "But they were dragged back out of sight as soon as they fell."

Before the captain could ask any more, the invaders spilled around the bend in the corridor like a flash flood filling a parched riverbed. As O'Connor had said, there were five or six of them, and they were firing green energy bolts.

Greenbriar couldn't see the aliens' faces, which were concealed inside black helmets with red-screened eye slits. However, there was no question that they were humanoid, with all the limitations and vulnerabilities that designation implied.

The captain took aim at one of the aliens and brought the beggar down, and Sasaki dealt a second one a glancing blow to the shoulder. But a moment later, O'Connor was slammed into a bulkhead, the victim of an enemy blast.

Greenbriar fired into the invader's midst while he still could—but before he could tell if he had hit anything, they were on top of him, overpowering him.

The captain used what he knew of hand-to-hand tactics, but the aliens' weight pinned him to the deck, and their helmets made it difficult to hurt them. Meanwhile, he had no such protection. While one of the bastards held him down, another one bludgeoned him with the barrel of his weapon.

Greenbriar felt as if he were falling end over end, the taste of blood thick in his mouth. Then, all at once, he regained control of his senses.

But it came with the knowledge that a second blow would be following the first. *If you don't succeed at first, try again.* The captain braced himself for the impact, clenched his jaw against it. But it never came.

Opening his eyes, he saw a corridor choked with bodies, only some of them those of his crewmen. And there were other crewmen kneeling among them, still alert and alive.

"Are you all right, sir?" one of them asked. It was Grolsch, one of the security officers who had arrived weeks earlier. "Do you understand me, sir?"

"Hell, yes." Greenbriar propped himself up and looked for his phaser. He found one nearby, though it could as easily have been O'Connor's or Sasaki's. Laying claim to it, he dragged himself to his feet and faced Grolsch on rubbery knees.

"Report," he demanded.

"They're all over the place," said the security officer. "And more are appearing all the time."

As if to lend emphasis to Grolsch's contention, Greenbriar heard the thud of heavy footfalls from somewhere down the corridor. He saw Grolsch and his fellow survivors exchange looks.

"Sounds like too many," said one of them.

"We've got to get out of here," said the other.

Grolsch turned to Greenbriar. "Sir?"

It was then that the captain realized he wasn't going to win this one. The odds were stacked too high against him. It was just a matter of time before the aliens overran his ship.

The realization changed things. He no longer hoped to contain the invaders. His goal now was to get a message out to Starfleet—to let them know what had happened to the *Cochise,* so they could formulate some kind of plan.

Because if the aliens could do this to *his* ship, they could do it to a hundred others.

"Well," said Urajel, "you were right."

Bender was accompanying her friend to engineering before she herself reported to the science section. "You mean about Ulelo," she said.

"Yes," said Urajel, her Andorian antennae bending forward. "You said he couldn't have committed the crimes of which he was accused. And as it turns out, he didn't."

"He just thought he did," said Bender, unable to keep a sigh out of her voice.

Urajel tilted her head to get a better look at the science officer. "Aren't you happy about that?"

"Happy that he's insane?" Bender asked.

The engineer dismissed the idea. "Happy that he hasn't transmitted our specs to anyone."

Bender swore beneath her breath. "I'm happy for *us,* sure. We're safe and secure. But what about Ulelo?"

The science officer wasn't sure which bothered her more—the fact that her friend was psychologically impaired, or the fact that she hadn't had the sensitivity to perceive it.

Maybe a little of both, she decided.

It killed Bender to know that Ulelo was sitting in the brig at that moment, as lost as a little child. He had seemed so capable to her, so comfortable in her company. A little reserved, maybe—more so than she remembered from their Academy days—but lots of people were like that.

She wished someone would tell her that Ulelo was going to be all right. However, she knew that might not happen. Medical science had come a long way in its ability to repair the body, but the mind was a different story. It was still mysterious in many ways, still incompletely understood.

Poor Ulelo, she thought.

"Listen," said Urajel, "I feel the same thing you're feeling. I wish Ulelo were well. But it's not as if there's anything we can do about it."

But there was, Bender thought. She couldn't cure him of what was ailing him, unfortunately. But while he remained on the *Stargazer,* she could let him know he still had a friend.

Greenbriar watched the turbolift doors slide open, revealing the sparking, smoking chaos of his bridge. It was empty but for four figures—Hohauser, Bolaris, Cangelosi, and Moy—all of whom had their phasers trained on the captain.

"Stand down," said Greenbriar, in case someone was too blinded by the smoke to recognize a friend.

His officers lowered their weapons. Moy, whose head cut was bleeding profusely, slumped back in his chair and groaned.

"How are things down below?" asked Hohauser, his face streaked with soot from the smoke.

"Bad," said Greenbriar, moving toward Moy and the com console. "The aliens are in charge there."

"What are we doing about it?" asked Bolaris, his tone too much like a challenge.

The captain shot him a glance. "We're consolidating our forces and trying to hold the more strategically important decks. And we're maintaining the decorum expected of Starfleet officers."

The Andorian recoiled. "Sorry, sir."

"No need to apologize," said Greenbriar, fighting off a wave of vertigo—a lingering effect of the blow he had taken earlier. "Just do your job."

Putting a hand on Moy's shoulder, the captain thanked him silently for his courage. Then he laid his phaser down on the com console and began entering a message to Starfleet Command.

He had barely gotten through the first sentence when Bolaris shouted a warning. Looking up, Greenbriar saw a blinding-white glow in the center of the bridge, and a handful of man-sized figures taking shape inside it.

They're beaming in here too, Greenbriar thought.

Bolaris and Hohauser poured energy fire into the glow. So did the security officers who had come up with the captain.

As he picked up his phaser to do the same, he saw a second glow, and a third—and the aliens in the first group were firing even as they fell. Greenbriar gave up whatever thoughts he had had of sending a message from the com panel. His people weren't going to be able to hold the bridge long enough.

But he had to get his message off. He couldn't let the aliens take the *Cochise* without warning the fleet.

Fortunately, there was another way. While his

officers tried to beat back the invaders, Greenbriar abandoned the com panel and returned to the turbo-lift.

He had almost reached it when an energy beam went sizzling by his ear and scorched a bulkhead. Casting a glance back over his shoulder, he saw that one of the aliens was getting ready to fire at him a second time.

But Cangelosi was quicker. Her phaser blast caught the invader in the shoulder and turned him around. That gave the captain time for a shot of his own, which sent the alien flying.

He wished he had time to stay and fight, but it wouldn't be possible. Swinging himself into the turbo-lift, he punched in a destination and plastered himself against one of the compartment's interior walls. Then he trained his weapon on the space between the closing doors.

Come on, he thought, urging the doors to come together faster.

An energy beam sliced past him and struck the back of the compartment, leaving it a blackened mess. But Greenbriar himself remained unharmed. And a moment later, the doors slid closed, allowing him to release the breath he had been holding.

As the turbolift began to move, Greenbriar wiped perspiration from his forehead with the back of his free hand. *With luck,* he thought, *there won't be quite so many of the invaders on deck seven.*

That was where his quarters were. And in them, he would find his computer terminal, which he could use to bypass the com station on the bridge and transmit a subspace message.

The captain had been in the turbolift for less than thirty seconds when the control readout told him he had reached his destination. He took a deep breath, waited until the doors slid apart, and stuck his head out.

No sign of an invader in either direction. *So far, so good.*

Edging out into the corridor, Greenbriar moved briskly in the direction of his quarters. As before, the curve of the passage cried out for caution. However, time was his enemy. There was no doubt that the invaders would catch him eventually. He just needed to get his message off first.

With every step he took, he expected to find an adversary lying in wait for him. But he didn't see any. Unbelievably, it looked like he would reach his quarters uncontested.

As the captain's door appeared around the bend of the corridor, there was still no one in sight—neither an invader nor one of his own crewmen. It was too good to be true.

Placing his hand over the metal security plate on the bulkhead, he triggered the mechanism that would give him access to his quarters. As his door slid aside, he took a last look in either direction.

Still no one, Greenbriar reflected. Remarkably enough, his luck was holding.

Entering his quarters, he waited until the door had whispered closed behind him. Then he went to his computer terminal, put away his phaser, and began telling the story of how the aliens had taken his ship.

He was almost finished when he saw a gob of reflected light appear on his monitor screen. His heart pumping, he grabbed his phaser and whirled about.

It was the same bright, white glow the captain had seen on the bridge. And in its midst, there were the same sort of shapes, taking on definition more swiftly than he would have liked.

Grabbing his phaser, he pointed it at the glow and began firing. At first his beams passed through the invaders, because they weren't substantial enough to absorb the impacts. But when they turned material, Greenbriar started to get results.

The first one doubled over and collapsed. The second went lurching into a bulkhead. And the third, who actually managed to get an errant shot off, nearly had his head wrenched from his shoulders.

Three up, three down. The captain would have been satisfied with the outcome if he hadn't seen the beginnings of another glow hovering beyond his monitor.

This time, he didn't fire into it—not right away. He made use of the few seconds he had left to finish his account, including as many details as he could. Only after he depressed the stud that would send it off did he grasp his phaser again and look up.

By then, the invaders were material enough to fire at him. Ducking, Greenbriar saw his terminal explode in a spasm of directed energy. Then he squeezed off a shot of his own, punching the nearest alien in the ribs.

He hit the next one too, taking his feet out from under him. But he missed the third one—and the alien didn't give the captain a second chance.

The invader's energy blast nailed him square in the solar plexus, feeling like a bolt of hot, heavy metal. It drove all the air from his lungs, leaving him gasping for breath, though somehow he managed to keep from losing consciousness.

At least for the moment. But as his vision cleared, he saw the alien take aim at him a second time.

Bastard, he thought.

Then Greenbriar felt the kick of the invader's beam, and fell headlong into a cold, black pit.

Chapter Seven

PICARD SAT BACK in his center seat and considered the yellow-orange disk of Delta Campara on his viewscreen.

"We're getting some impressive readings," said Wu, who had come to stand at his side.

"No doubt," the captain replied. "It is, after all, one of the larger Cepheid variables in Federation space."

"With some spectacular prominences," Wu added.

"Yes. Quite spectacular." He frowned. "I don't suppose they are appreciatively different from the prominences observed by Captain Crajjik twenty-five years ago?"

The second officer hesitated. "We've only been studying Delta Campara for a few hours."

"Six," said Picard. "And thirteen minutes. And have we observed anything Captain Crajjik did not?"

"Well," Wu said with obvious reluctance, "no."

Picard nodded. "Wherein lies the problem."

"Look at the bright side," said Wu. "In another couple of days, we'll be finished here."

That was indeed the bright side. But by then, McAteer would have some other busywork lined up for them. And beyond that, Picard had a hearing to look forward to.

"A brave attempt," he told Wu.

"But you're not cheered," she noted.

"Not significantly, no."

"Sir?" said Paxton from his place at the com station.

Picard turned to him, hoping that Paxton had something more interesting to offer than Delta Campara. "Yes, Lieutenant?"

"It's Admiral Mehdi calling from Command, sir. He's asking to speak with you—in private."

Mehdi? the captain wondered. He hadn't heard from the admiral in months. "I will take it in my ready room," he said. Then he got up from his seat and made his way into his sanctum.

In a matter of moments, Mehdi's narrow, pinched face was staring at him from his computer screen. Even on his good days, the admiral wasn't a particularly congenial man—but at the moment, he looked positively grim.

"Jean-Luc," said the admiral.

The captain inclined his head. "Sir."

"We've got a problem," said Mehdi, as succinct as ever. "In the last few hours, two of our starships—the *Cochise* and the *Gibraltar*—have been attacked by unidentified assailants."

Picard understood now why the admiral had looked so solemn. "Their status?" he asked.

Mehdi shook his head. "We don't know. They both got off distress calls, but we haven't heard from them since."

It wouldn't have been good news no matter which ships were involved. But the *Cochise* was commanded by Denton Greenbriar, one of the canniest captains in the fleet—and Picard's friend since their involvement in the White Wolf incident.

Mehdi scowled. "There's more. The *Antares* hasn't responded to our hails for more than a day now. It's our guess that she's been attacked as well."

The captain's throat was suddenly very dry. "Admiral, I dispatched a shuttle to meet the *Antares,* with Admiral McAteer aboard. And six of my crew."

Only Mehdi's eyes reflected his sympathy. "All the more reason to find out what happened to her—and quickly."

"You want the *Stargazer* to investigate her disappearance?"

"Exactly. I'm transmitting a set of coordinates—the last known position of the *Antares.*"

Indeed, Picard saw the coordinates appear in white characters in the lower right-hand corner of the screen, superimposed on the image of the admiral.

"You're to get there as soon as you can," Mehdi continued, "and let us know what you find out. We need to get a handle on who's carrying out these attacks and why, before they decide to take another shot at us."

"And my shuttle?"

"Is a secondary concern right now. I'm sure you understand."

"Of course," said Picard, however reluctantly. The *Antares* had to come first.

"Further instructions will be forthcoming," said the admiral. "Good luck, Jean-Luc. Mehdi—"

"Wait," said Picard, as a possibility occurred to him. Mehdi stared at him. "Yes?"

The captain's mind raced. *Ulelo.* He had transmitted the *Stargazer*'s specs—to no one in particular, if Greyhorse was right about the com officer's state of mind.

But what if Ulelo's transmissions had been purposeful after all? What if someone had received them and studied the technologies employed by the *Stargazer*? Someone who might have been daunted by Federation firepower for some time—and now had the knowledge to wade through a starship's defenses as if they weren't there?

The *Cochise,* the *Gibraltar,* the *Antares* . . . they were all *Constellation*-class, like the *Stargazer.* Their specs would all be the same. Picard felt the blood rush to his face as the the pieces began falling into place. . . .

"Admiral," he said, "I may be able to shed some light on what happened to our ships." And he went on to tell Mehdi about Ulelo, his transmissions, and the conclusion reached by Picard and his staff. "However, considering what you've told me about the *Cochise* and the other vessels . . ."

"You think Ulelo may not have been so crazy after all."

"I do," said the captain.

"And where is Ulelo now?"

"In the brig—where he will remain, at least until we determine the truth of the matter."

"See that he does," said Mehdi. "In the meantime, I'll alert the rest of the fleet that our adversaries may know our ships as well as we do."

Obviously, he wasn't happy about the prospect. However, he also wasn't blaming Picard for it.

"Now," said the admiral, "I have even more reason to wish you good luck. Medhi out."

As the older man's visage faded from the screen and was replaced by the Federation insignia, Picard sat back in his chair. He felt as if someone had kicked him in the stomach.

He felt personally responsible for the Ulelo situation. He had been content to accept the notion that the com officer was out of touch with reality, and that his actions had ultimately been harmless.

Now, it appeared, Ulelo's actions might have consequences after all—deadly ones. For all the captain knew, the lieutenant had placed the entire Federation in danger.

And Ben Zoma's team on the shuttlecraft was as vulnerable as anyone. If something had happened to the *Antares,* the *Livingston* might be next.

Picard felt an urge to go after his people, to reel them in. But Mehdi's instructions didn't leave him much wiggle room. He was to look for the *Antares*—period.

"Picard to Idun Asmund," he said, making use of the ship's intercom system to contact his helm officer.

"Aye, sir?" came the response from the bridge.

"We are altering course." And he gave her the coordinates he had received from Mehdi.

"Acknowledged," said Idun.

Next, Picard summoned Wu and Greyhorse, in

order to discuss Ulelo with them in more depth. Then he contacted Paxton and apprised him of their orders.

"Send a message to the shuttle," said the captain, "and let Commander Ben Zoma know what is going on."

"Of course, sir," said Paxton.

Picard sat back in his chair. Before long, he assured himself, the *Livingston* would be headed for the nearest starbase—McAteer wouldn't brook any other course of action. Then the shuttle would remain there until the danger had passed.

That was by far the most likely course of events. Of course, there were other possibilities—grimmer ones—but there was no point in the captain's worrying about them.

Especially when he suddenly had so much else to worry about.

Ben Zoma was going over the shuttle's latest sensor reports when he heard someone forward of him swear under his breath.

Looking up, he saw Horombo shaking his head over the com panel, where Ben Zoma had stationed him. The security officer was obviously unhappy about something.

Joining him, Ben Zoma said, "Something wrong, Mister Horombo?"

Horombo unfolded himself from his chair and pointed to his subspace message monitor. "Take a look for yourself, sir."

Sitting down in Horombo's place, Ben Zoma inspected the monitor. There was a message from Captain Picard on it. As the first officer read it, he came to understand why Horombo had reacted as he did.

By then, they had drawn the attention of the rest of the crew. "What's going on?" asked McAteer, voicing the question that must have been on all their minds.

Ben Zoma turned to him. "Apparently, a couple of our ships have been attacked and boarded."

The admiral's eyes narrowed. "Which ones?"

"The *Cochise* and the *Gibraltar*," said Ben Zoma. "And the *Antares* isn't responding to hails, so there's a possibility she was attacked as well."

"The *Gibraltar?*" asked Chen.

"That's right," said the first officer.

Chen swallowed, and didn't say anything more— but Ben Zoma knew why the security officer had asked the question. He had a brother on the *Gibraltar*.

McAteer looked as if he had consumed something rotten. "Who attacked them?"

"No one knows," said Ben Zoma. "Which is why the *Stargazer* has been dispatched to conduct a search for the *Antares*—so we can get some answers."

Garner's brow knit above the bridge of her slender nose. "If the *Antares* is missing, and the *Stargazer* is on a mission to find her . . ."

"Then we've got no one with whom to rendezvous," said McAteer, finishing the security officer's thought.

"So where do we go?" asked Ramirez.

Ben Zoma wished he were the one empowered to decide their next move. But he wasn't—not as long as McAteer remained the highest-ranking officer on the shuttle.

Turning to the admiral, the first officer said, "Sir?"

McAteer shrugged. "I don't think we've got any choice, Commander. We'll report to the nearest starbase." He glanced at Paris. "That would be One-Two-Nine, I believe?"

The helm officer confirmed it.

"After all," McAteer went on, "this is a shuttlecraft, not a starship. If the *Cochise* and the *Gibraltar* weren't able to stand up to our mysterious enemy, I doubt there's much *we* can do."

Ben Zoma had some ideas about that. But, knowing how futile it would be to voice them, he kept them to himself.

Picard gazed across his desk at Wu and Greyhorse. They looked back at him with the same expectant look on their faces, obviously wondering why he had summoned them.

He didn't leave them in suspense.

"Two of our starships—the *Cochise* and the *Gibraltar*—have been attacked by unidentified vessels," he said. "And we've lost contact with the *Antares.*"

"When did this happen?" asked Greyhorse.

"Command received the distress calls less than an hour ago. And though the fates of the *Cochise* and the *Gibraltar* are still unknown, both captains spoke of defending against boarding parties."

Wu's otherwise flawless brow creased with concern. "What about our shuttle?"

"I have sent Commander Ben Zoma a message notifying him of the attacks. With luck, he will receive it in time to move the *Livingston* out of harm's way."

Greyhorse frowned. "Why can't we meet the shuttle ourselves?"

"Admiral Mehdi has assigned us to investigate the fate of the *Antares*. Besides, the *Livingston* is probably seeking the shelter of a starbase by now."

Silence reigned for a moment, as Wu and Greyhorse digested the information. Then the second officer spoke up.

"Whoever attacked them must have had some pretty impressive firepower," she observed. "Greenbriar and Rodriguez are both formidable combatants."

Picard leaned forward. "Unless the intruders knew our tactical systems inside and out. Then they could have worked out a way to pierce our defenses."

Greyhorse looked at him askance. "But how would they have that kind of—" He stopped in midsentence. "You're not suggesting that Ulelo had something to do with this?"

"I am," said Picard. "I no longer believe that Ulelo was carrying out a schizophrenic fantasy. I believe he was transmitting data to a group of aliens, who used it in their attack on the *Cochise* and the other ships."

Again, his officers took a moment to mull what he had said. This time, it was Greyhorse who reacted first.

"It may yet turn out to be a coincidence," he said.

"It may," the captain conceded. "But if it is, it will be a rather large one. On one hand, Ulelo repeatedly transmits data to an unknown party. On the other, an equally unknown party attacks our vessels with remarkable success. It is not much of a leap to suspect that there is a connection."

Greyhorse sighed. "Perhaps not."

The captain turned to Wu. "Do you think Ulelo is capable of shedding light on our attackers?"

The second officer frowned. "He couldn't even keep straight whom he was working for. I doubt he can be of any help to us, even if he's willing." She looked from one of her colleagues to the other. "Still, I suppose I can give it a try."

Picard nodded. "Please do."

Nikolas was ensconced in the *Iktoj'ni*'s small, badly ventilated operations center, running a routine diagnostic on her deflector array, when he heard the clatter of approaching footfalls in the corridor outside.

"Nik?" someone called, his voice echoing wildly.

It had to be Locklear. No one else on the cargo hauler called him by that name. For that matter, no one on the *Stargazer* had called him Nik either.

Not even Obal.

Nikolas's thoughts turned to the Binderian, as they had almost every day since he set foot on the cargo hauler. And as always, he set them aside.

Obal was a relic of the life Nikolas had put behind him. He was part of the past, like Gerda Idun. And Nikolas owed it to himself to look to his future.

"I'm in here," he called back, keeping his eyes firmly fixed on his readouts.

"There you are," said Locklear, his voice closer now.

Out of the corner of his eye, Nikolas saw his friend

swing into the room. But then, Locklear's shock of red hair made him hard to miss, even obliquely.

"What's up?" asked Nikolas.

"You won't believe this."

Something in Locklear's voice made Nikolas turn to him. When he did, he saw the unmistakable expression of concern on his friend's face.

Locklear wasn't the type of person to get worried over nothing. If something was bothering him, it was a bigger item than, say, a glitch in his sonic shower.

"What's the matter?" Nikolas asked.

"While I was up on the bridge," said Locklear, "Captain Rejjerin received a message—from Starfleet, of all places."

That got Nikolas's attention. "Starfleet . . . ?"

"Yes. And it wasn't just to say howdy. Apparently, someone's attacking the Federation—or parts of it. But the message didn't say who was doing it or why. It just advised us to avoid the usual shipping lanes."

Nikolas whistled. "Rejjerin must be steaming. She promised she would get this cargo to Djillika on time."

"She still may," said Locklear. "I heard her say she refused to change course."

Nikolas looked at him. "You're kidding me."

"I'm not," said his friend. "She said she's got a schedule to keep and she'll be damned if she's going to let a few troublemakers scare her off."

Nikolas leaned back into his chair. "Great."

"Just what I was thinking."

"Any chance the captain will change her mind?"

"I've never known her to, but there's always

a—" He stopped himself in midsentence. "Nah. No chance."

"So, what do you think? A little mutiny?" Nikolas suggested with a straight face.

Locklear chuckled a little. "Mutiny's for your fancy Starfleet ships. Around here, we just grumble."

"Then grumble quietly," Nikolas recommended. "I've got a diagnostic to finish."

He didn't love the idea of ignoring a Starfleet alert and remaining on course for Djillika. However, it didn't look like he had much choice in the matter.

Chapter Eight

Picard was pacing the bridge of the *Stargazer* like a caged cat when at last he heard what he had been waiting for.

"Sir," said Gerda, "sensors have identified a vessel. It appears to be the *Antares.*"

Finally, the captain thought. "On screen."

A moment later, he saw the ship they had been sent to find. But she wasn't as Picard had seen her last. Then, the *Antares* had fairly bristled with power and grace. Now she was hanging in space, her hull dented and charred by what was clearly weapons fire, looking for all the world as if she had been abandoned. Even her observation ports were unlit.

"Life signs?" he asked, less than eager to hear the answer.

"Quite a few," said Gerda, much to Picard's relief. "Maybe as many as a hundred."

It was good news. The *Antares* had set out with a crew of a hundred and eight.

"Do they have power?" the captain asked.

Gerda called up another sensor report. "Barely. Enough to run life-support in a few parts of the ship."

That explained how Vayishra's crew had survived. But if the *Stargazer* hadn't arrived when she did, they might not have survived much longer.

"Try hailing them," said Picard.

There was no answer.

But then, communications might have been one of the systems damaged in the attack. And if the crew was restricted to certain areas, it would have been difficult to effect repairs.

"Commander Wu," he said, accessing the ship's intercom system, "this is the captain. We have located the *Antares*."

"What kind of shape is she in?" asked Wu.

"Not as bad as she might have been. I want you to take a team over. Identify the injured and have them beamed back to sickbay. Then assist the others in effecting repairs."

"Right away, sir," said the second officer, probably already on her way to the nearest turbolift.

Picard frowned. He was eager to hear what had happened in Captain Vayishra's own words—assuming the fellow was still alive.

*   *   *

Ulelo had been thinking for a long time about the period he had spent with his masters—thinking *hard*—when he realized there was someone standing in front of his cell.

And it wasn't Commander Wu, for a change. Much to Ulelo's surprise, it was his friend, Emily Bender.

Ulelo looked into her eyes and wondered how she would respond to what he had done. He wondered what she would say.

It was a moment he had attempted to picture long before his treachery was discovered. The prospect of his friend looking down on him as he sat there in the brig had almost kept him from transmitting the *Stargazer*'s specs.

Almost.

But Ulelo had gone ahead with his transmissions anyway. And now, much to his discomfort, he would have an opportunity to see if the reality of his present situation had anything in common with his expectations.

After a moment, Emily Bender was joined by Lieutenant Pfeffer, who tapped in the code that deactivated the electromagnetic barrier, and let Ulelo's friend into his cell. Then Pfeffer raised the barrier again and withdrew.

It left the prisoner alone with Emily Bender. Unlike the second officer, Ulelo's friend sat beside him on his bed. Her expression—one of sadness and uncertainty—almost made Ulelo wish that his visitor had been Wu after all.

But Emily Bender didn't say the sort of things he had dreaded to hear from her. When she finally spoke, her tone was unexpectedly kind and understanding.

"Are you all right?" she asked.

"I'm . . . fine," Ulelo told her.

She looked at him a moment longer. Then she said, "Whatever happened, Dikembe, I know it's not your fault. You would never willingly do what they say you've done."

He didn't know what she meant. He said so.

"If you sent those messages," Emily Bender explained, "you must have been under the influence of someone else. You must have been their puppet."

"Their puppet?" he repeated.

"Uh-huh. Is that what happened, Dikembe? Were you under somebody else's control?"

He didn't know what to say.

Emily Bender put her hand on Ulelo's. "It's all right, Dikembe. Just remember, I'm still behind you. *All* your friends are behind you. You're not alone in this."

She said other things as well, comforting things. But all the com officer could think about was the possibility that Emily Bender had suggested to him. . . .

"Is that what happened, Dikembe? Were you under somebody else's control?"

After a while, Emily Bender left, assuring Ulelo that she would be back. Pfeffer restored the electromagnetic barrier and the com officer found himself alone again.

And he had even more to think about than before— because he was no longer just trying to remember the time he had spent with his masters. Now he was also trying to recall why he had agreed to work for them.

But he couldn't.

He wasn't drawn to anyone else's way of life. He

didn't believe he owed anybody anything. And yet, he had felt compelled to do what had been asked of him, to the detriment of his comrades. He had felt it was a necessary endeavor—worth the price of his freedom, not to mention the trust of his friends.

He had been sure of that, if little else. *Absolutely* sure.

But now that he thought about it, he couldn't imagine *why* he had been so sure. And for that reason, he had to entertain the possibility that Emily Bender was right—that he had been manipulated against his will.

That he was, in her words, a *puppet.*

Avul Vayishra was a tall, darkly complected man with a black goatee. He had been one of Admiral McAteer's favorite captains from the day the admiral took over administration of the sector. McAteer had described Vayishra as a natural leader, a paragon of Starfleet efficiency.

But Vayishra didn't look like a paragon of efficiency at the moment. As he sat warming his hands around a steaming cup of coffee, he just looked stunned.

"They cut through our shields as if they weren't even there," he said, his voice thinned by cold and fatigue. "And when we fired back, our weapons barely slowed them down. There wasn't much we could do except try to hold on."

Picard, who was sitting opposite his colleague in an otherwise empty set of crewman's quarters, considered Vayishra's tale. It was very much in keeping with the distress calls transmitted by the *Cochise* and the *Gibraltar.*

"Unfortunately," said Picard, "I may have an explanation for the aliens' superiority." And uncomfortable as it was for him, he went on to describe Ulelo's activities.

Vayishra's eyes opened wide. "Do you know what you're saying? The magnitude of it? This could be *disastrous.*"

"I am aware of that," said Picard.

The other man looked vaguely accusatory. "I assume you've passed this on to Starfleet Command?"

"I have," Picard confirmed. "I alerted them as soon as I learned of the aliens' attacks."

Vayishra looked up at him. "There were others?"

"The *Cochise* and the *Gibraltar* seem to have encountered the same aliens you did. They managed to send out distress calls, but that was the last we heard from them."

"What about your shuttle? And the admiral?"

"I was just going to ask you the same thing."

Vayishra scowled into the depths of his cup. "I hope they got off easier than the *Antares.*"

So did Picard. He had hoped for good news, but at least he hadn't gotten any *bad.*

"It seems a miracle," he said, "that none of your crewpeople was killed."

Vayishra shook his head, a look of disgust taking over. "No. Not a miracle at all. If those aliens had wished to destroy us, they would have done it."

Picard empathized with Vayishra's pain. "Then what do you suppose they were after? Your cargo, perhaps?"

"We weren't carrying anything out of the ordinary," Vayishra told him. "And what we *were* carrying is still intact. The bastards didn't so much as pry open a canister."

"Your weapons, then?" Picard suggested. There was

a large, thriving black market for Starfleet ordnance. "Or some component of your propulsion system?"

"They left all of that untouched. Not that there was much left of value when they got through with us."

It was maddening. "So they crippled your ship, boarded it, and then left? There must be more to it."

"I'm sure there is," said Vayishra, with a hint of resentment in his voice.

Picard hadn't meant to offend anyone. "My apologies," he said. "I did not mean to imply that you were taking this lightly."

"Believe me," Vayishra continued, "it's not as if I haven't thought about this over and over again. It's been on my mind every waking minute."

"I believe you," said Picard.

Vayishra looked at him with dark, haunted eyes, and went on as if his colleague hadn't spoken. "But if there is a rational reason for what they did, I have yet to find it."

Picard just nodded.

"It wasn't my fault," Greyhorse whispered.

Gerda's expression, as she filled the entrance to his office, indicated that she disagreed. "You're a physician," she said, keeping her voice low enough so that no one elsewhere in sickbay could hear her. "You examined Ulelo. And you came to the conclusion that he was acting out a fantasy—which we now know was very real."

"But I'm not a counselor," Greyhorse complained. "I don't have any training in psychodynamics—I told the captain that. He just refused to listen."

"You were asked to rise to the occasion," Gerda snapped, "and you failed. Miserably."

Miserable was how the doctor felt—and not just because Gerda was reviling him. He had given the captain, and in a sense the entire fleet, a false sense of security—one that might eventually end up costing them the Federation.

No one could be sure that a warning would have saved the *Antares* or any of the other ships that were attacked, or that it would have put the fleet in a better position. But by the same token, no one could say otherwise.

It was a terrible feeling—like a knife in his gut, always twisting. But as deep as it cut, Gerda's disapproval cut even deeper. She was a Klingon, after all, in every way but blood. She didn't look kindly on failure, or those guilty of it.

"A warrior doesn't make excuses," said Gerda. "It only makes things worse."

Greyhorse's mouth clamped shut. But if he couldn't explain what had happened, how could he regain her trust—her confidence? How could he restore himself in her eyes?

The answer was as clear to him as the rank of biobeds behind Gerda, which were full of sedated crewmen from the *Antares:* He *couldn't.* He could only hope for a chance to prove his courage.

"Will I see you later?" he asked, dreading the answer.

She didn't say anything. She just stood there, her eyes narrowed in high contempt. And after a moment or two, she left.

"It wasn't my fault," Greyhorse whispered, though there was no one left to hear it.

But of course, it *was*.

Having returned from the *Antares*, Wu was on her way to the brig to speak with Ulelo again when she heard someone call her name. Looking back, she saw that Lieutenant Bender was trying to catch up with her.

"Can I speak with you a moment?" Bender asked.

"Of course," said the second officer. She gave some thought to the most convenient place. "My quarters?"

"Sure," said Bender.

A turbolift ride later, they were sitting in Wu's ante-room, looking at each other across a bamboo coffee table. "What did you want to speak about?" asked the second officer.

"Ulelo," said Bender, "what else?"

What else indeed.

"I just spent some time with him," said Bender, "and something occurred to me. If he sent out those transmissions, which I still can't believe, he couldn't have done it of his own volition. Someone had to have programmed him."

Wu weighed the possibility. It made as much sense—or as little—as any other theory she had considered. "I don't suppose you have any proof of this?"

"Not a shred. But if you know Ulelo, it's the only explanation for what he's done."

"Well," said Wu, "I *am* interested in why Mister Ulelo did what he did. However, I'm more interested in the people those transmissions were meant for."

"The captain asked me about them too," Bender noted, "but I still don't have a clue. Ulelo doesn't seem to be able to keep them straight in his mind."

Unforunately, Wu knew that from experience. But maybe that would change this time. Maybe Ulelo would shed some light on the Federation's mysterious assailants.

And help to undo some of the damage he had done.

Chapter Nine

Ulelo was a little disappointed when Wu came to visit him. He had hoped it would be Emily Bender again.

No—it was too soon for that, he told himself. Emily Bender had just been there a few minutes earlier. She probably wouldn't come back for some time.

"How are you?" Wu asked, once she had sat down with Ulelo on his side of the electromagnetic barrier.

"Fine," he told her. "And you?"

"To be honest," she said, "I've been better. Some of our ships have been attacked."

Ulelo was concerned. "Was anyone hurt?"

"We're not sure," said Wu. "We don't know who did it, either. The ships in question have stopped communicating."

That didn't sound good.

"All we know," Wu continued, "is that the attackers

have an advantage over us—some kind of tactical superiority that allows them to defeat us at every turn."

"I'm sorry to hear that," said Ulelo. Who wouldn't be?

His visitor regarded him for a moment. "As I say, we don't know any more than that. But we've made some guesses. You know those transmissions you made?"

He nodded. "Yes."

Wu leaned forward. "We think that's where our enemy's tactical advantage came from. We think they took the information in those transmissions and used it to make their weapons more effective against us."

Ulelo felt the blood drain from his face. *His* transmissions had allowed them to do that? But he had sent them to his masters, not a bunch of hostile aliens.

He told the second officer that. But it didn't seem to make her feel any better.

"Mister Ulelo," she said, fixing him with her gaze, "your masters and those hostile aliens . . . they're one and the same."

The same? he wondered. How could that be? His masters weren't enemies of the Federation. They had no reason to launch attacks on Starfleet vessels . . . *or did they?*

Ulelo licked his lips as the question echoed inside him. If his masters hadn't planned on using the information he gave them to attack the *Stargazer*'s sister ships, what the devil *were* they going to use it for?

He didn't think anyone had ever told him. And he also didn't think he had ever asked.

But now that he thought about it, it made sense that they would use his transmissions against Federation ships. It made *perfect* sense. So why had it never occurred to him before? What was wrong with him that he hadn't seen it?

Ulelo had known that he was betraying his friends by transmitting that data. But he had never considered the extent of that betrayal. He had never asked himself if what he was doing might get someone hurt—or even killed.

Emily Bender had asked him if he was being controlled by someone—if he was a puppet. The more he considered the possibility, the more he wondered if she might have been right.

But even if it were true, it didn't absolve Ulelo of what he had done. It didn't render him blameless. Starships had been attacked, entire crews placed in deadly jeopardy. They were his responsibility, all of them.

His.

He imagined the remains of a starship floating in space, corpses and spindrifts of blood expanding from one end of the debris field to the other. He wanted to wipe the scene from his mind, but he couldn't. Helplessly, he watched the dance of death. . . .

"Mister Ulelo?" said Wu.

He looked up, suddenly relieved of his torment, and saw that the commander was watching him.

"Do you understand what I'm saying?" she asked.

He did. Or at least he thought he did—it was so hard for him to think at the moment.

"It would help a great deal," said Wu, "if you could tell us more about the people we're dealing with."

"Of course," he said, eager to lend a hand. He started to describe his masters—and then stopped.

It was strange. Ulelo could still picture them, but he couldn't find the words he needed to speak of them. He couldn't even attach a name to them. *You named them before,* he thought—and he had. But try as he might, he couldn't name them now.

It made his pulse race. Commander Wu needed his help. How could he fail her this way?

The second officer frowned. "Maybe something will come to you. If it does, I hope you'll let me know."

"I will," he promised. And he would. Just as soon as he could get himself to remember. . . .

"Any luck?" Picard asked.

Wu, who was seated on the other side of his desk, shook her head. "I don't believe so. Ulelo seems to regret what he did, but he's still not giving me anything to go on."

The captain stroked his chin. "I wish we at least knew *why* he did it. That might illuminate everything else."

"Actually," said Wu, "Lieutenant Bender's got a theory about that. She believes Ulelo was programmed."

Programmed, Picard repeated inwardly. *Like an automaton, dedicated to serving a distant puppet master.*

"It would explain a lot," he conceded.

"Unfortunately," said the second officer, "there is no way to prove it. At least, not conclusively."

The captain shook his head. It would help if he knew when Ulelo had become involved with whomever he served. Months ago, perhaps, when he was on shore leave with the *Polaris,* his previous posting? If that were so, he could have been transmitting information even before he came to the *Stargazer.*

For all Picard knew, there were moles like Ulelo scattered throughout the fleet, each one assigned to a different starship. Some of them might be com officers, some of them engineers, some of them science officers. And unlike Ulelo, they would still be free to collect information.

It occurred to Picard that he should share this thinking with his fellow captains. He needed to warn them that there might be spies on their vessels as well . . .

Before the situation got any worse.

Two days into the *Iktoj'ni*'s passage through the sector Starfleet had warned them about, violence erupted. But it wasn't the kind Nikolas had expected.

It started in the corridor between the main cargo bay and the engine room. Nikolas and Odzig, a lean, narrow-faced Skezeri, had just finished repairing a dead spot in the gravity grid. They were on their way to repair another one when they passed two other crewmen.

One was a human, a redheaded female named Shockey. The other was Kroda, a Tellarite with a lavish beard and a large, proud snout.

Nikolas didn't see the intitial contact between Odzig and Kroda. But before he knew it, they were going at it, shoving each other back and forth.

"Hey," said Nikolas, "what's going on?"

"This burden-beast thinks he owns the corridor!" Odzig snapped, his already protuberant eyes looking as if they were about to explode from his head.

"Keep your bony hands off me," Kroda bristled, "or I'll snap them off at the wrist!"

"Stop it!" said Shockey, forcibly wedging herself between the combatants. But she didn't see the flash of something metallic, as Nikolas did.

Not certain who was holding the blade, he took a chance and lashed out at the Tellarite. Unprepared for the blow, Kroda staggered and slumped against the bulkhead.

Without Kroda in the way, Nikolas could see that it was Odzig who was holding the knife. Exposed, the Skezeri tried to conceal it again, but Shockey grabbed his arm.

"Back off!" Odzig rasped, trying to pull away from the woman.

"Not a chance," Shockey told him. "You know we're not allowed to keep weapons on the ship."

"Let it go!" Nikolas warned the Skezeri, believing that a warning would be enough. After all, Odzig had seemed like a decent enough guy on their repair detail, the kind who would see reason if given half a chance.

But far from relinquishing the blade, Odzig tore free of Shockey and lifted his weapon as if he meant to slash her with it. Unable to wait any longer, Nikolas lowered his shoulder and launched himself into the Skezeri.

They went barreling down the corridor end over end, both of them scrabbling wildly for Odzig's weapon. Nikolas felt something sharp and fiery bite into his ribs. Then he got hold of the blade's handle, twisted it away from the Skezeri, and threw him backward into the bulkhead.

"That's enough!" Shockey barked.

Everyone stopped. Nikolas, Odzig—even Kroda, who was getting to his feet. They glared at each other, their breath coming fast, but no one went after anyone else.

The Skezeri wiped some spittle from his mouth with the back of his hand. "I wasn't going to use it," he told Nikolas. Then he turned to Shockey. "You should have left me alone."

"So you could poke holes in Kroda?" she asked. "I don't think so."

Nikolas tucked Odzig's knife into his belt. Then he reached under his shirt and felt his ribs where the knife had gotten him. It stung where he touched them. But when he looked at his fingertips, there was hardly any blood on them.

Kroda turned to the Skezeri. "You cut him!"

"Barely," said Nikolas.

"Let me see that," said Shockey.

Keeping an eye on Odzig, Nikolas lifted his shirt. He felt the woman's touch, gentler than he would have expected. She made a sound of dismissal.

"It's nothing," she said.

"But it *could* have been," the Tellarite pointed out.

They looked at each other for a moment. Then Shockey spoke up again. "I'd advise everyone to go about their business and forget what happened here. Unless someone has an objection, I'm going to take the knife and dispose of it."

"How?" asked Odzig.

"That's my business," she told him.

The Skezeri seemed reluctant to protest any further,

and Kroda didn't protest at all. As far as Nikolas was concerned, Shockey could do what she liked with the knife. He didn't want any part of it.

Odzig looked at Nikolas like a kid who had done something wrong and didn't want to admit it. "Come on," he said. "We've got a repair to make."

"You go," said Shockey. "He'll be along."

The Skezeri scowled at the idea, but accepted it. Straightening his shirt, he continued down the hall. And a moment later, Kroda trundled off as well, leaving Nikolas and Shockey standing there by themselves.

He drew the knife from his belt and gave it to her. Then he said, "You're really going to keep this to yourself?"

"Damned right I am." She looked at him askance. "This your first haul or something?"

"As a matter of fact, it is."

She didn't comment on it, but her disdain was palpable. "Come with me," she said. "I'll bandage that so you don't bleed through your shirt."

He went along without comment. As they walked, Shockey said, "Odzig wasn't lying about the knife, you know. I really should have left him alone."

"You think so?" asked Nikolas.

"Definitely. He's not a bad sort. Under normal circumstances, he wouldn't have flown off the handle that way. But this waiting, this constant peering out observation ports to see if a ship is bearing down on us . . ." Her jaw muscles worked. "It's driving all of us out of our minds."

It was a tense situation, no two ways about it. Nikolas had tried to put it from his mind, and succeeded for the most part. But it appeared to be taking its toll on his crewmates, even more so than he would have imagined.

Unfortunately, things weren't going to change in the near term. The captain wasn't going to turn the ship around. She had made that plain enough.

After all, they were in the heart of the danger zone. It wasn't going to help them to come about. The fastest way to find safe harbor now was to hew to their original course.

And hope their luck held out.

Picard was in his quarters, pulling on his captain's uniform after a fitful night's sleep, when he heard his name called via the ship's intercom system.

Looking up, he said, "What is it, Mister Paxton?"

"Sir," said the com officer, "they've located the *Gibraltar.*"

Picard tamped down a surge of apprehension. "What sort of shape is she in?"

"Nearly all her systems have been compromised, sir. But there were no fatalities. All hands are alive."

Just like the Antares. The captain breathed a sigh of relief.

"These aliens . . ." he remarked, "if they're conquerors, they're remarkably accommodating."

"It seems that way," agreed Paxton.

And now they knew even more about Federation starship technology, since they had had an opportunity to examine a few specimens firsthand. If the invaders had been formidable before, they might be even more so now.

But why did they need to attack *three* ships to serve their purposes, when all three were of the same class and design? Wouldn't one vessel have satisfied them?

And why *not* destroy the ships of their enemy, as long as they had the chance? By refraining, the aliens had merely increased the odds against them.

It was baffling. And unless the Federation found a way to stand up to the aliens, it might never become less so.

"Any word on Ben Zoma and the others?" he asked Paxton.

"None, sir," came the response.

Under the circumstances, Picard didn't know if that was good news or bad. However, he continued to take solace in the knowledge that the *Livingston* hadn't reached the *Antares* yet when the starship was attacked. That meant the shuttle might still be free. . . .

At least for the time being.

Ernesta Rodriguez of the *Starship Gibraltar* felt a sharp pang of loss as she surveyed her bridge.

Everything was dark—the forward viewscreen, the helm and navigation consoles, the aft stations on either side of the turbolift. And she could have left it that way, with the shadows created by the wide beam of her palmlight only suggesting the damage that had been done there.

But she didn't want to. It was important to her that she examine everything, that she absorb the sight of it and file it away for future use.

So Rodriguez narrowed her palmlight's beam and traced a path, starting with the bulkhead to her left and working her way around, illuminating each section of the bridge in turn.

When she got to the helm console, she stopped for a moment. The enemy's very first barrage had turned it into a fountain of flames and sparks, forcing the captain to switch to auxiliary helm control—and send her helm officer to sickbay with third-degree burns. Now the console was a slag heap, cold and twisted and useless.

Rodriguez stopped again when she got to the engineering station, which was set into the bulkhead aft of the navigation controls. There was a blotch of dried blood there where Cherry, her first officer, had careered headfirst into the metal-alloy surface.

And she hadn't been able to get him to sickbay right away, because he got hurt while the enemy was taking control of the bridge. It wasn't until after the aliens were gone that Rodriguez and her weapons officer were able to get Cherry some care.

In the meantime, the *Gibraltar* had been left adrift—blinded, silenced, and paralyzed. None of her systems were working except a couple of backup generators, and they were barely enough to maintain life-support.

Of course, it could have been worse. In the end, everyone had survived. And as badly as the enemy had incapacitated the ship, the crew had still managed to get the com system on line.

Without it, they would have been looking forward to another day, maybe more, before a rescue vessel could locate them. As it was, Captain Reynolds and the *Zhukov* would reach their coordinates in a matter of hours.

It wasn't that Rodriguez wasn't grateful for these things. It was just that she thought of her ship as a friend—a very old and dear friend, after fourteen years of sitting in her center seat—and the captain hated to see her gutted this way.

It made her want to strike back at the ones who had done this, to punish them for what they had done. Unfortunately, the *Gibraltar* was in no shape to accommodate her wish. Besides, there wasn't any reason to think a second clash with the enemy would produce better results than the first.

Rodriguez still didn't understand how it had happened. No adversary had ever slipped her phasers that way, or eluded her torpedoes, or pierced her deflector shields. But this enemy had done all those things.

And yet they weren't nearly as impressive in close-quarters combat. They weren't especially strong or fast, and their hand weapons didn't seem to have either the range or the accuracy of Starfleet's phaser pistols.

The only reason they managed to take over the ship was that they outnumbered the defenders. Had it been an even fight, the crew would have prevailed—Rodriguez was certain of it.

But why had the enemy attacked at all? Not to destroy the *Gibraltar,* certainly, or to make off with crew or cargo or even data. The computers had been pretty much disabled by the time the aliens beamed aboard.

Then why had they bothered? To avenge some slight of which Rodriguez was unaware? Or to test their military strength against that of a starship, in preparation for a bigger move—maybe a full-scale invasion?

She wished she knew.

"Captain?" said a voice behind her.

Turning, she saw that it was Baskind, her chief engineer. His face was a mask of soot and grime, but he was smiling through it.

"Good news?" Rodriguez asked.

"I'd say so," Baskind replied. "We found some sensor records from the time of the attack."

She looked at him disbelievingly. "They weren't destroyed?"

"Not all of them, apparently. The sonuvaguns missed a few." He turned over the padd he held in his hand. "As you can see, we got some interesting readings."

They were interesting, all right. Apparently, the ship that attacked them hadn't been alone. It was just the front-runner in a far-flung quintet of ships, four of them arranged in a diamond shape twenty kilometers long.

And unless Rodriguez was mistaken, the vessel bringing up the rear wasn't even a warship. It was too massive, too unwieldy, for the invaders to take into battle.

Because the ships were so far apart, the crew of the *Gibraltar* had noticed only the one attacking them. But it was clear now to Rodriguez that the aliens were adhering to a formation—a distinctive one, unlike any she had seen before.

If they remained in it, Starfleet might be in luck. It could pinpoint the aliens' location with long-range scans, and maybe prevent them from attacking anyone else.

"Good work," she told Baskind. "Command will want to see this as soon as possible."

His smile widened. "I had a feeling you'd say that. Why don't we send it to them right now?"

The captain agreed that that would be a good idea. And anyway, she had accomplished what she had set out to do when she came up to revisit the bridge.

Accompanying Baskind into the turbolift, she punched in engineering as a destination. That was where they had resurrected the com system, and it was still the only place on the ship where they could gain access to it.

Rodriguez looked at the padd again. They needed information like this if they were going to beat the invaders the next time—and she couldn't imagine that there wouldn't be a next time.

"Place is a mess," said Baskind, "isn't it?"

Rodriguez looked up at the bridge again and nodded. Then the lift doors closed and they descended toward engineering.

Ben Zoma was thinking about his cousin Dahlia, whose colony was less than a light-year off the course Admiral McAteer had selected, when Garner got his attention.

"Sir," said the security officer, from her seat at the control panel beside Paris, "I'm receiving another message. This one is from Starfleet Command."

Ben Zoma glanced at the admiral, who had mercifully seen fit to doze off in the rear of the craft. Rather than wake him right away, the first officer would see what the message was about.

Moving forward, he took a look at it. It was a compilation of data, everything Starfleet had managed to gather on the enemy—including the whereabouts of his vessels, to the extent that they could be determined.

And it hadn't just been sent to the *Livingston*. According to the signature on the message, it had been transmitted to the entire fleet.

"Interesting," said Ben Zoma.

"What is?" asked McAteer, whose eyes had coincidentally chosen that moment to open.

"The enemy seems to be advancing in units of five vessels apiece. But only four of the vessels in each unit are warships. The fifth is a much larger, ungainly-looking affair, which lags behind and seems to function as a supply drone."

Ben Zoma turned to look at the others. "No need to carry extra food, spare parts, or reusable energy resources. The supply ship does that for them."

"So they travel fast and light," the admiral observed, "rendering them more effective in combat. Makes perfect sense, if your only objective is a military one."

"But it wouldn't work for *us*," said Horombo, "because we're explorers as well."

"Maybe it's not an ideal situation for them either," said Ben Zoma, thinking out loud.

McAteer leaned closer. "What do you mean?"

The first officer frowned. They were behind the enemy's line of attack. From all appearances, they were safe.

But one of the invaders' five-vessel units was still within a billion kilometers of them. It wouldn't be difficult to catch up to its supply drone.

With a little care, Ben Zoma and his people might

be able to slip aboard the vessel, hide there, and then sneak onto a warship in the midst of a supply transfer. That would give them a chance to reconnoiter, examine their adversaries' systems up close, and possibly identify a few weaknesses.

Clearly, the enemy knew how to take apart a starship's defenses. With a bit of luck, they might be able to help Starfleet return the favor.

"What I mean," the first officer said, in answer to the admiral's question, "is that the enemy may have given us an opportunity."

And he described his idea to the others.

"Mind you," he added, "it's a dangerous proposition. There's no guarantee it'll succeed—or that we'll still be alive to celebrate if it does. But Captain Picard and our friends on the *Stargazer* are risking their lives to defend the Federation. I don't see why we shouldn't do the same."

Paris and the security officers seemed willing enough. But Ben Zoma had to consider McAteer, who had already decided that they should proceed to the nearest starbase.

The admiral's eyes narrowed and remained that way for several seconds. Then he spoke.

"I like it."

The first officer looked at him, wondering if he had inadvertently stepped into an alternate reality where McAteer was a reasonable man. "You do?"

"Absolutely," said McAteer. "It's far from a certain thing, of course. But our duty to the Federation demands that we make the attempt, regardless of the odds."

Ben Zoma couldn't believe the admiral had gone along with his plan. However, he wasn't about to look the proverbial gift horse in the mouth.

"Ensign Paris," he said, "come about and head for the supply vessel. Best speed."

Paris turned back to his controls. "Aye, sir."

Ben Zoma watched the stars wheel across the shuttle's observation port. Finally, they stabilized, a sign that he and his crew were pursuing their new course.

He would have liked to send a message to the *Stargazer,* letting Picard know what they intended, but he couldn't take the chance that it would be intercepted and deciphered. It was a risky enough venture even without that.

In fact, Ben Zoma couldn't remember the last time he had taken this big a chance, or had so much riding on how he fared. *Rolling the dice,* he told himself, as he settled back in his seat and steeled himself for what was ahead.

Chapter Ten

FOR PERHAPS THE FIFTIETH TIME since they had made the
decision to change course, Ben Zoma watched Admiral
McAteer drift over to the shuttle's control console.

Craning his neck over Chen's shoulder, the admiral gave their navigational monitors the once-over.
"How's it going?" he asked the security officer.

"Fine, sir," said Chen.

"Good," said McAteer. He turned to Paris, who was
manning the helm again. "You?"

"Good here too, sir," said the ensign.

The admiral nodded. Then he stretched a bit, as if
that had been the main purpose of his excursion, and
returned to his seat in the aft part of the vessel.

Once Ben Zoma was sure that McAteer was behind
him, he smiled to himself. The admiral was obviously
one of those people who just didn't feel comfortable

delegating responsibility. It was a wonder that the man had come up so far through the ranks, considering how difficult it was to accomplish anything in Starfleet without putting some faith in one's subordinates.

Ben Zoma believed he understood now why McAteer's relationship with Picard had been so rocky. If the admiral had a hard time trusting people, he would be that much less inclined to place his trust in a rookie.

The first officer, on the other hand, was perfectly content to get some rest and let Chen do his job. So, apparently, were Ramirez, Garner, and Horombo, who were tilted back in their seats and sleeping soundly.

Ben Zoma shut his eyes too. After all, he didn't know what they would encounter on the aliens' supply vessel. It might be a long time before he got another chance to sleep.

One moment, Ulelo was in the *Stargazer*'s brig, gazing miserably at yet another in a long string of security officers through the sizzling haze of a confining energy barrier.

The next, he was beset by images he couldn't quite grasp. Images that nagged at him as if he should know them, but remained just beyond the pall of his conscious mind.

An expanse of fissured, black earth stretching to a double sunset of pale gold. A dense, azure forest, the underbrush giving off its own light in the otherwise impenetrable gloom of tree-shadow. A bloodred tide pawing insistently at a shoreline of dazzling, diamond-dust beaches.

And a dozen other sites, each more unfamiliar and unlikely than the one before it.

He hadn't seen these things on any Starfleet mission. He was reasonably certain of that. But the memories were so vivid, so real as they clung to the edges of his vision, that he was certain he had seen them *somewhere,* on some occasion he couldn't seem to dredge up in its entirety.

Finally, after torturing himself for hours, Ulelo believed he knew where he had seen the fissured plain, and the azure forest, and the bloodred tide. *On the planet of the people he had worked for.* It had to be.

He didn't remember being prepared for his mission on the *Stargazer,* but he *must* have been. Otherwise, how would he have known what to do, or how to go about it? And it made sense that his preparation would have taken place on his masters' homeworld.

Yes, he told himself for perhaps the hundredth time—for the more he said it, the easier it was to embrace. His masters' homeworld, a place so alien, so unlike anywhere else . . .

Where what seemed like a carpet of soft, white ground cover was actually an army of tiny, vicious predators. Where rust-red pellets fell from the sky in savage twists of wind, only to shatter on piles of gray-and-white striped rock.

He had no way to confirm it, no way to put his mind completely at ease. But if he had to decipher what was happening in his brain, this was the answer he felt most comfortable with.

And Ulelo needed an answer of some sort, needed it

even more than food and water. Because without it, he was afraid he would go insane.

Nikolas was stretched out on his bed in the quarters he shared with his friend Locklear, going over everything he had to do the next day, when he heard the harsh buzz that told him someone was waiting outside his door.

If he were still on the *Stargazer,* he could have admitted whoever it was with a simple voice command. But as he was reminded a hundred times a day, he wasn't on the *Stargazer* any longer.

Swinging his legs out of bed, Nikolas got up and went to the door, then pressed a black pad set into the bulkhead. A moment later, the duranium panel hissed open, revealing his caller.

It was Redonna, the ship's primary pilot—a black and white striped Dedderac with large, dark eyes and a spare if well-muscled frame. Nikolas hadn't had occasion to speak with her previously, other than to ask her to pass a condiment in the mess hall. He wondered what she had come to tell him.

"Well?" said Redonna.

Nikolas looked at her. "What?"

"Aren't you going to invite me in?"

"Sure," he said.

Obviously, what she had to tell him was going to take longer than she cared to stand in the corridor. Moving aside, Nikolas let her into the room.

There weren't any chairs because there wasn't enough space for them. As a result, Redonna took a seat on the corner of the human's bed, propping her leg up and lying back against the bulkhead.

"What can I do for you?" he asked.

The pilot regarded him. Then she said, in a voice huskier than those of most Dedderac, "You don't seem very concerned about the danger we're in."

He had to smile at the unexpected nature of the remark. "Is that how it looks?"

"Most everyone in the crew is walking around with a weight on his neck. But not you. Why is that?"

Nikolas shrugged. "I don't know. I guess I don't see the point of worrying about it."

Redonna nodded. "That's pretty much the way I look at it. But I grew up smuggling disruptor rifles, so I'm used to sticking my nose where it doesn't belong."

Her nostrils flared, a sign of amusement in a Dedderac. Obviously, she hadn't entirely hated the smuggling life.

"But you weren't a smuggler," she noted. "I'd know if you were. So why doesn't it bother you that we're taking a chance?"

It was because Nikolas had served in Starfleet, where exposure to danger was practically an everyday occurrence. But he didn't tell Redonna that.

Captain Rejjerin knew where he came from, and so did Locklear. But no one else, and he wanted to keep it that way. Otherwise, he would have to get into an explanation as to why he had left the fleet, and that was the last thing he wanted.

Redonna tilted her head. "Hiding something, are we? I wonder what it could be." She looked him up and down. Suddenly, something seemed to come to her. "Rings of Tultarri . . . why didn't I see it from the beginning? You were a uniform, weren't you?"

He frowned. "I don't—"

"You worked for Starfleet," said the pilot, making it sound like something dirty. "Admit it."

Nikolas didn't answer. He just kept frowning, stalling until he could think of something.

"Don't worry," said Redonna, "I won't give away your little secret." Her nostrils flared again, even wider this time. "I've got a secret too, you know."

"Oh?" said Nikolas, his curiosity aroused.

"Yes. You see, I've been monitoring your schedule and Locklear's for some time now, waiting for a moment when I could catch you alone in here."

Nikolas's heart started to beat a little harder. Was Redonna doing what he thought she was doing?

She put her hand to the front of her throat and caressed it with her fingertips. Then she dropped them a little lower and unfastened the topmost snap of her tunic, exposing a prominence analogous to a human collarbone and a little more of her perfect, striped flesh.

"You see," Redonna said, her voice a little more languid now, a little more sinuous, "I've had my eye on you since the minute you beamed aboard."

She leaned forward and grabbed a fistful of his shirt. Then, stronger than she looked, she drew him down to her.

"It gets lonely on a cargo hauler," Redonna whispered. "But there are ways to relieve the loneliness."

Suddenly Nikolas felt her mouth on his, her lips soft

and warm, her breath redolent of something sharp and fragrant. And part of him was tempted to give in, because he was lonely too.

Then, in his mind's eye, he saw Gerda Idun—sleeping like a child as the hours approached morning, her golden hair spread like a fan across his pillow. And the idea of being with anyone else became inconceivable to him.

In that moment, he pulled away from Redonna—and saw the surprise in her eyes. But it didn't stay there long. It was quickly replaced with cold, sharp-edged anger.

"You don't like me?" she spat.

"It's not that," said Nikolas. "It's—" He felt he had to give her some taste of the truth. "There's someone else."

Redonna glared at him for a second. Then her mouth twisted into a sneer. "I hope she's worth it, Starfleet. You don't have any idea what you're missing."

Then she thrust him away, got up from his bed, and headed for the door. Pounding the pad set into the bulkhead, she waited until the panel slid open. Then, without a look backward, she stalked off into the corridor.

Nikolas sighed. He had left the *Stargazer* to forget Gerda Idun, to put her behind him with the rest of his past. But even here she continued to dog his steps, to haunt him with the memory of her beauty.

Falling back on his bed, he closed his eyes and wondered if he would ever be free.

Ben Zoma was in the process of dozing off when he heard Horombo call his name. Blinking away sleep, he joined the security officer at the navigation controls.

By then, McAteer was up and about as well. He

peered over Horombo's shoulder as he had peered over so many others.

Ignoring him, the first officer asked, "Got something?"

"I believe I do, sir," said Horombo.

"Slow to impulse," said Ben Zoma.

"Impulse," Paris confirmed.

Suddenly, the stars froze around them. No longer vivid streaks of light, they were simply tiny points now, insistent but static.

However, they hadn't traveled all this way just to gaze at the neighborhood. Ben Zoma watched Horombo check his monitors for additional data on the supply ship.

"Is it what we came for?" asked the first officer.

"It sure seems like it," said Horombo.

Ben Zoma smiled. "Distance?"

"Fifty thousand kilometers."

The first officer was about to ask Horombo to put their objective on a screen. But at that distance, they would be within visual range in a matter of seconds.

"There she is," said Paris, pointing forward.

Ben Zoma took a peek through the observation port. So did McAteer, getting between Paris and Horombo in the process.

What they saw was daunting, to say the least.

The vessel was colossal, several times the size of the *Stargazer* and dark gray in color. Its long, angular hull boasted eight small nacelles, their mouths all glowing with a fierce vermilion light.

None of the warships it served were visible. However, the sensors were registering their presence, the nearest one being almost two hundred kilometers up ahead.

"Life signs?" asked McAteer.

"None that I can detect," said Horombo.

"I think I see a cargo bay," said Chen. He pointed to a rectangular outline on the drone's port side.

"I don't know what else it could be," said Horombo.

"We can try to get in that way," said Ben Zoma. "But I'd prefer to find a docking port. Then we've got a shot at manual access."

"I think I found one," Ramirez announced from an aft station. "And here's another, on the other side."

The first officer went back to see what Ramirez was looking at. Sure enough, there was a much smaller outline that suggested a docking facility.

He turned to his pilot. "Mister Paris, you'll stay with the admiral. The rest of you will—"

"The *hell* he will," said McAteer.

Ben Zoma looked at him. "Sir?"

"I have no intention of hanging back in this shuttle, Commander. If you're going to try this, you're going to do it with the benefit of my experience."

The first officer didn't know how good an idea it was to include the admiral on the away team. Even if McAteer had once been a crack ship's officer, it was a long time since he had put himself on a bull's-eye. He might get into trouble and drag the rest of them down along with him.

"Sir," said Ben Zoma, seizing on the first angle that came to mind, "this is going to be a pretty dangerous proposition. I'd be remiss in my duty if I put the life of a superior officer in jeopardy."

McAteer smiled a sour smile. "Not if that superior officer insisted on it—which I do."

There wasn't much that Ben Zoma could say to that. The decision had been taken out of his hands.

"All right," he said. He turned again to Paris, who had watched the exchange with interest. "You might as well come too. We can put the shuttle on autopilot."

"Aye, sir," said the ensign. But it was clear that he was glad to be going along.

And Ben Zoma was glad to have him. It would be helpful to have another capable officer at his disposal—especially when he would constantly have to keep one eye out for McAteer.

Picard stood in the engine room of the *Antares,* studying a vaguely hourglass-shaped warp core that was identical to that of the *Stargazer* right down to the last stem bolt. It was shimmering inside with a ghostly, blue light, looking every bit as vigorous as it should have.

"Well," Picard observed with satisfaction, "it appears that you are back in business."

"That it does," said Captain Vayishra, who was standing beside him, his aquiline features softened by the glare. "But if you hadn't come along, the *Antares* would have been as dead as the invaders left her."

And you and your crew along with it, thought Picard. But he refrained from mentioning that unhappy detail.

"We were pleased that we could help," he said instead.

Vayishra looked as if he meant to say something

more. However, he was interrupted by the voice of his com officer, which Picard had by then heard often enough to recognize as easily as his own.

"Captain," said the officer, "I have Admiral Mehdi. He wishes to speak with both you and Captain Picard."

The two men exchanged glances. Vayishra seemed to be of the same opinion as Picard—that they wouldn't appreciate what they were about to hear.

"Patch it through to the main engineering console," said Vayishra.

"Aye, sir," said the com officer.

Picard and Vayishra moved to the console in question. It was in the same place as the one used by Simenon on the *Stargazer.* A moment later, Mehdi's image appeared on a monitor screen. He looked as if he hadn't been sleeping very well.

"Good news?" Picard asked hopefully, despite the admiral's appearance.

"I wish it were," said Mehdi.

Do not tell me that something happened to the shuttle, Picard insisted silently. Please *do not tell me that.*

"Two more of our ships have been attacked," Mehdi reported. "The *Ojanju* and the *Gettysburg.* Both of them managed to send out warnings to the fleet before they fell incommunicado."

Picard absorbed the information.

"Judging by the coordinates of the attacks," the admiral continued, "our adversaries are steadily moving toward the heart of the Federation. They'll reach Earth in a matter of days if we don't stop them."

Picard understood the significance of Mehdi's observation. However, it was Vayishra who expressed it out loud.

"It's been more than a hundred years," he said, "since an enemy has gotten within firing range of Earth."

And back then, Picard noted, there was significantly less at stake—the fate of a single planet, not an entire union of worlds. If Starfleet Command were destroyed, the damage to the Federation would be incalculable.

"Command has decided that we'll make a stand," said Mehdi, "with all the firepower we can muster. The *Antares,* I understand, is in no shape to fight. . . ."

"However," Picard inferred, "the *Stargazer is*—and you want her to be part of the effort."

"What I want," said Mehdi, "is for you to be off studying worlds we've never seen before, looking for new forms of life and undiscovered civilizations. But under the circumstances, yes, I'd like you to be part of the Federation's defense."

Picard nodded. "Consider it done, sir."

Mehdi fashioned a halfhearted smile. "Thank you, Captain. I'll transmit the pertinent coordinates."

Picard didn't like seeing the admiral this way. He seemed to be carrying the weight of the entire Federation on his narrow shoulders. "We will stop them," the captain blurted, attempting to sound as reassuring as possible.

Mehdi appeared to brighten a bit. "I trust you're right," he said. He looked around. "I've grown rather fond of this place. I'd hate to lose it."

And his image vanished from the screen.

"This place," said Vayishra, echoing the admiral's words. "I wonder if he meant his office . . . or Earth."

It was an ominous question. Picard didn't have the stomach for answering it. Neither did Vayishra, apparently.

Picard turned to his colleague. "I hate to leave the *Antares* to her own devices."

"Don't worry," said Vayishra, "we'll manage. It's the *Stargazer* I'm concerned about."

Picard regarded Vayishra, wondering what, exactly, the fellow intended by his remark. After all, he was an ally of McAteer. Was he implying that the *Stargazer*'s captain wouldn't be equal to the task in front of him?

"We'll manage as well," he said, unable to quite keep the indignation out of his voice. Then he started for the exit.

"Picard," said Vayishra.

Picard stopped and turned. "Yes?"

"All I meant was that you'll be on the front line. Nothing else, I promise you."

Picard took the remark at face value. "Thank you," he told Vayishra. Then he turned again, and left engineering for the nearest transporter room.

Chapter Eleven

ELIZABETH WU WAS LYING on her bed, staring at the ceiling of her quarters as if she might somehow find all the answers she wanted from Ulelo displayed there.

She ran her conversations with him over and over again in her mind, sifting them for just a nugget of something she could use. But it was to no avail.

The second officer was so intent on her introspection, she barely heard the chime that announced someone at her door. And she had a sinking feeling that it wasn't the first time it had rung.

Getting up from her bed, she left her bedroom behind and emerged into the adjoining anteroom. Then she said, "Come in."

As the doors opened, Wu saw that it was Jiterica. The ensign was looking remarkably like a humanoid in her new, improved containment suit. But if the look on the ensign's face was any indication, she was anxious about something.

"Good to see you," said Wu. She indicated a chair on one side of the room. "Please, have a seat."

"Thank you," said Jiterica.

Not so long ago, she would have found it painfully awkward to sit down. Her new suit seemed to have eliminated that problem.

"Is everything all right?" Wu asked.

Shortly after Jiterica came on board, the second officer had appointed herself the ensign's unofficial guardian. Back then, Jiterica was lonely and unsure of herself, uncomfortable in an environment built for higher-density beings.

Fortunately for Jiterica, that had all changed, and she didn't need a guardian as much as she used to. However, Wu had yet to relinquish the position.

"It's Ensign Paris," said Jiterica.

Ah yes, thought Wu. *Paris.*

Jiterica and her fellow ensign had become rather close over the last couple of months. And the second officer, who harbored a liking for both of them, had been delighted to see how much they enjoyed each other's company.

Of course, there was that brief period where Paris appeared to want to avoid Jiterica, when he had pulled back from her. It had bothered Wu to see it, almost to the point where she had said something to him.

But thankfully, that phase had passed, and Paris and Jiterica had become constant companions again. So it was perfectly understandable if Jiterica was concerned about her friend.

"You want to know about the shuttle," Wu concluded.

"Yes," said Jiterica. "Has there been any word?"

Wu wished she had better news. "Not yet."

Clearly, the ensign wasn't pleased. "Shouldn't we have received a message by now, either from another ship or from a starbase?"

The second officer nodded. "Perhaps we should have. But I'm not going to jump to conclusions. Unless I hear something to the contrary, I'm going to assume Commander Ben Zoma and his crew found safe haven."

Jiterica took a moment to consider the remark. "You believe they're uninjured?"

"I do," said Wu.

The ensign smiled. "Then I will believe that too."

Wu was gratified that Jiterica placed such faith in her. She just hoped that when it came to the *Livingston,* neither of them found a reason to be disappointed.

On the Cargo Hauler *Iktoj'ni,* Nikolas eyed the plate in front of him, which was heaped high with slender, pale tubers drowned in thick, black sauce.

"It's better than it looks," Locklear assured him from his seat on the other side of the table.

"I don't see how it could be worse," said Nikolas.

The cargo hauler wasn't equipped with the state-of-the-art replicators that had become standard on Federation starships. The one they had wasn't able to work fast enough to create a variety of dishes every night, so they had it make mass quantities of the same dish instead.

This evening, it was a Fayyenh specialty that Nikolas couldn't even pronounce. Translated, it was rays-of-sunshine-in-old-dark-mud. Somehow, he wasn't tempted by it.

It occurred to him that if he left it alone for a while and came back to it, it might not seem quite so unappealing. Pushing his chair away from the table, he looked around the mess hall.

The captain, a Vobilite, was discussing something with a couple of her mates on the other side of the room. Like all of her ruddy-faced species, Rejjerin had to speak around the curved tusks that protruded from the corners of her mouth, a condition that made her look argumentative sometimes.

But not this time. As she sat there trading remarks, she seemed confident, relaxed—and for a good reason. The *Ik'tojni* had nearly cleared Starfleet's danger zone. In another day at their present speed, they would be home free.

Of course, there was still a chance that the captain would come to regret her decision. But to that point, it looked like she had made the right one.

"She's something, isn't she?" asked Locklear.

Nikolas saw that his friend was studying Rejjerin as well. "I guess you could say that." He didn't think Captain Picard would have taken that kind of risk—not unless there was a lot more at stake than a cargo delivery.

Locklear chuckled. "I remember how nervous you were when I told you the captain was forging ahead."

"No," said Nikolas, "actually that was you."

His friend looked at him, his brow creased down the

middle. "Now that you mention it, maybe it was. Anyway, I'll be damned if her luck isn't holding."

Nikolas couldn't argue with the facts. "I just hope our next job takes us somewhere far from this danger zone. I don't think I'd want to push Rejjerin's luck *twice.*"

Locklear turned a little pale beneath his freckles. "Amen to that."

Nikolas took a fresh look at his dinner plate. Unfortunately, it didn't look any more appealing than it had before. If anything, it looked less so.

It almost made him wish that the mystery marauders would show up after all. That way, he wouldn't have to eat the stuff.

Ben Zoma watched the alien vessel's docking port loom nearer and nearer, until it was so close that he could see the scratches on its hatch plate.

Only then did he say, "Ease her in, Mister Paris."

"Aye, sir," said the ensign. Then he turned the shuttle sideways and gently applied port thrusters to nudge her toward her target. After a moment or two, he married one surface to the other with a metallic thunk.

Unfortunately, the shuttle's door didn't fit the docking port precisely, and anything less than a perfect accommodation would leak dangerous amounts of oxygen. However, Starfleet's engineers had long ago foreseen such an eventuality.

Using a separate set of controls in the corner of the console, Paris extended a flexible seal around the docking port. Then he reinforced it with a transparent

electromagnetic barrier, not unlike the one used in the
Stargazer's brig.

Ben Zoma put a hand on the ensign's shoulder. "Are
we good?"

"We are," Paris confirmed.

"Good work," said the first officer. Then, glancing
at the others, he said, "Don suits and check phasers."

It took a couple of minutes for everyone to do that.
As it happened, McAteer took the longest. But then, it
had probably been years since he even looked at a containment suit, much less confirmed the charge in a
phaser pistol.

"Ready?" said Ben Zoma, his voice sounding tinny
as it came to him over his helmet's receiver.

Everyone nodded in their helmets. Even the admiral,
though he was the highest-ranking officer aboard and
could have led the mission himself, if he had wanted to.

"All right," said Ben Zoma. And he depressed the stud
on the control panel that would open the shuttle door.

As it slid aside with a soft exhalation, it revealed the
supply vessel's hatch cover, which had six sides and was
made of the same dark metal alloy as the rest of the ship.
There was something protruding from it that was clearly
intended to be a handle, indicating that the aliens had
appendages not a great deal unlike Ben Zoma's own.

He turned to Chen, then Ramirez. "Open it."

The two security officers slipped their phasers into
the appropriate slots on the exterior of their suits. Then
they advanced to the hatch door and bent to the task of
turning its handle in a counterclockwise direction.

Of course, it might not have been designed to rotate

in that direction. It might not have been intended to rotate at all. But it certainly seemed to be the required approach.

For a moment, nothing happened, leading Ben Zoma to wonder if their expectations had led them astray. Then finally, the handle turned, and they heard a distinct clunk—suggesting that the hatch's locking mechanism had disengaged. Chen and Ramirez looked at each other, then pulled.

With a slight puff of equalizing gas pressure, the hatch door swung open. As Ben Zoma had anticipated, there was an airlock beyond it—dimly lit and cylindrical in shape—and a similar door on the far side.

Hunkering down, he entered the lock. Then he gestured for the rest of the team to follow. When they were all inside, Chen and Ramirez pulled the hatch door closed behind them and relocked it with an interior handle.

A moment later, Garner and Horombo started working on the opposite hatch. This one yielded more easily than the first, perhaps because they were turning it with more confidence.

As the hatch swung aside, all Ben Zoma could see beyond it was darkness. He stuck his head through the opening and confirmed it—nothing but darkness in every direction. But then, the ship was unoccupied. Why waste energy on illumination when there was no one there to benefit from it?

Activating his palmlight, Ben Zoma took a few quick stabs at the place. It seemed immense. His beam traveled a long way before it finally hit something solid.

And even then, it wasn't a bulkhead. It was a sprawling terrain of squat, cylindrical containers. But that was good news. It meant they were in the vessel's main cargo hold.

"Come on," Ben Zoma said. "Let's take a look around." And he moved out into the benighted expanse.

One by one, the others followed—first McAteer, then Paris, and finally the security officers. Their palm-lights sliced through the darkness like knives through fat, dark flesh.

Fortunately, the soles of their containment suits were soft and padded, unlike the soles of their boots. Otherwise, they would have announced themselves with every echoing footfall.

Not that there was anyone there to hear them. But eventually, there would be. At least, that was their hope.

Ben Zoma checked his tricorder. The news it gave him could have been a lot worse.

"Heat," said Garner, reading off her own device.

"And breathable air," Horombo added.

"Don't get too comfy," Ben Zoma warned them. "That could all change in a heartbeat."

Ramirez was nodding. "I was on a space station once where the humidity content of the air went from twenty-five percent to ninety percent every ten hours, to accommodate the needs of the species that had built her."

"They should have made up their minds," said Garner.

Ramirez chuckled. "You can say that again."

Ben Zoma liked the banter. It kept them loose. On a mission of such importance, that could only be an asset.

Seeing nothing that might deter them from pursuing

their plan, the first officer turned to Paris and said, "All right, Ensign. You can let her go."

"Aye, sir," said Paris.

He looked a little reticent to comply. It was understandable, considering he was the member of their team who had piloted the *Livingston* and therefore knew her the best.

On the other hand, her continued presence outside the supply ship was a danger to them, as she would alert the enemy that there was someone within. Removing a remote-control device from a pocket of his suit, Paris closed the *Livingston*'s door. Then he disengaged her and sent her on her way.

It left them alone in the alien supply vessel, without a way to get off it in the event of a problem. But with luck, they would have another way to get off soon enough.

Picard was standing in front of his captain's chair, hands clasped behind his back as he watched the stars shoot by on his viewscreen. *Not much longer now,* he thought.

"Sir," said Gerda, "I've got them on sensors."

Picard didn't turn around to face her. He didn't have to, already knowing what she was talking about. "On screen," he said.

The steady stream of stars vanished. And in their place, there were starships—a great many starships. Most of them resembled the *Stargazer.* A handful had the sleek, dynamic look of the *Excelsior*-class. And a few others were modeled after the larger, more powerful *Ambassador* prototype, still being perfected in the fleet yards at Utopia Planitia.

Picard had seen many of them at one time or another, in orbit around a starbase or at some rendezvous point. However, he had never seen them all in one place, amassed side by side against the backdrop of space.

He glanced at the monitor and read the list to himself. The *Jor'fasi,* named after the great liberator of the Vobilites. The *Victory.* The *Magellan.* The *Hathaway.* And a couple dozen others, with additional reinforcements still on the way.

They had gathered at these coordinates for one reason, one very important purpose—to defend the Federation. And in most cases, Picard would have felt confident in such impressive company. But not in *this* case. Not when the aliens had demonstrated an ability to plow through a starship's defenses as if they were no more durable than spiders' webs.

En route, Picard had received a message from Admiral Mehdi. Captain Sesballa, the Rigelian who commanded the *Ambassador*-class *Exeter,* would be giving the orders when they joined battle with the invaders.

Sesballa had distinguished himself in one of the Federation's last clashes with the Romulans, more than two decades earlier. He had achieved success several times since then, even earning a medal or two, but it was his performance against the Romulans for which he was still remembered.

Picard had never met the fellow, but he had studied Sesballa's tactical philosophy back at the Academy. It was conservative, methodical, an approach the young

Picard had found distinctly unappealing. However, he couldn't argue with Sesballa's track record—not then and not now.

It came as no surprise that Starfleet Command had placed Sesballa in charge of the defense formation. He had more experience than anyone else there, and he commanded more respect from his peers. Had Greenbriar been present, the job might have fallen to him instead. But with the *Cochise* crippled and far away, Sesballa had to be considered the next best option.

"Hail the *Exeter,*" Picard said.

A moment later, a ruby-eyed Rigelian appeared on the viewscreen. The corners of his mouth were lifted in something like a grin, though his tone was anything but merry. "Sesballa here," he said. "Welcome to the front, Captain."

"Thank you," said Picard. "I have been told that you will be calling the shots. Do you have a preference as to where I deploy the *Stargazer?*"

"For now," said Sesballa, "no. We can deal with that after I see who joins us and what we've got to work with."

"Did you receive my communication?" asked Picard, keeping his question vague for the benefit of Sesballa's bridge officers. "The one concerning my officer?"

"I did," said Sesballa. "And I have discussed the matter with the other captains here. To this point, none of us has experienced a similar problem."

That was good news, at least. "Nonetheless," said Picard, "we should continue to monitor the situation."

Sesballa nodded his hairless, silver head. "My

thought exactly. We will speak again, Captain." And he signed off.

Once again, Picard found himself looking at the defense formation. He turned to Wu, who had come up to join him.

"None of them have rooted out an informant," she said. "But that doesn't mean they don't have any."

The captain shrugged. "Captain Sesballa said they would continue to investigate."

Of course, there was the possibility that Ulelo had been one of a kind—the only informant in the entire fleet. If that were so, Picard had to marvel at the fate that had placed such an individual on the *Stargazer,* and the *Stargazer* alone.

Ben Zoma would have worn himself out ribbing his friend about it. *Only you, Jean-Luc.*

Frowning at the viewscreen, Picard wondered where his first officer was at that moment. On a starbase, he hoped—somewhere safe, somewhere far from the aliens' pattern of incursion.

Of course, if the invaders continued to have their way with Starfleet's finest, no place in the Federation would be safe for much longer.

Ulelo sat in his cell and kept his eyes closed as long as he could. That way, he could avoid distractions and focus on the images assailing his mind—the images that seemed more important to him now than ever before.

Because he wasn't just seeing places anymore. Now he was seeing *people* in those places. In the forest, at the diamond-dust shore, on the parched, black plain . . .

Some of them were engaged in activities Ulelo readily understood, running a race or collecting leaf samples or some such thing. But others were doing things he didn't understand at all, things that didn't look the least bit familiar to him.

And—this was the strangest part of all—the people he saw in his visions didn't look alien to him. They looked like *humans.*

Why should that be? he asked himself. Were there others like Ulelo in those places, dedicated as he was to serving the aliens who lived there? Had he seen them at some point? *Known* them?

Had those other humans gone back to their starships as he had, their missions much the same as his? Were they serving on their ships even now, operating undercover as he had operated undercover—unaware that Ulelo had been apprehended by his crewmates and incarcerated?

Not that he could do anything about it. He was penned up in the brig. He had no way to contact any-one, to tell them that they were doing wrong.

But what really troubled him wasn't the possibility that there were others like him, transmitting data on other starships. It was what had troubled him all along—the fact that he couldn't remember for certain, one way or the other.

That morning, as he woke from sleep, he thought he had caught a glimpse of the truth that had been eluding him—an image that looked back at him squarely, rather than sliding past the corner of his vision. It was a human, like himself, but a female. She was in a room, not unlike Ulelo's quarters on the *Stargazer.*

And she was speaking to him. He couldn't hear her, but he could see her mouth moving. She was trying to tell him something—something *important,* judging by her expression.

But for the life of him, Ulelo couldn't figure out what it might be.

Chapter Twelve

IT WAS ONE THING to survey the vastness of the aliens' cargo bay from the vantage point of an airlock. It was another to walk around the perimeter of the place, dwarfed by its immensity.

The architecture had a vaguely serpentine look to it, with repeating patterns of twists and scales. It was made of what appeared to be metal, but in the glow of their palmlights it had the iridescent sheen of oil in sunlight.

None of them had ever seen anything like it. They said so, freely commenting on what they observed.

Certainly, the level of insight would have been greater if Ben Zoma were exploring the ship with a team of exobiologists. However, Starfleet security officers weren't exactly slouches when it came to understanding alien cultures. They usually knew exactly what they were looking at—or could at least make an educated guess.

Ben Zoma knew that as well as anyone, having served as the *Stargazer*'s security chief once upon a time. It was Picard who had promoted him to first officer when a Nuyyad attack unexpectedly made the slot available.

"This is one hell of a structural integrity field," Garner said, running her tricorder over the bulkhead.

"It has to be," said Horombo. "As big as this thing is, the stresses on it must be enormous."

"The technology seems about the same as ours," Chen observed.

"Seems that way," Ramirez agreed. "But they've got many more emitters per meter."

Every ten meters or so, they came to another collection of supply containers. Each one was different. In one, the containers were tall and thin, in another short and wide. Sometimes there were just a few of them, and sometimes there were dozens.

Their contents varied as well. In most cases the tricorders registered machine parts, but they also came across what appeared to be foodstuffs, or perhaps medicines.

"I'd rather have a replicator," said Ramirez.

"They might have those too," Paris pointed out. "This could just be raw material—something they break down and use."

"Or an alternative," said Garner.

"Or a supplement," Chen suggested.

Only McAteer remained silent. In fact, he hadn't

said a word since they put on their suits back in the shuttle. His expression, visible through his faceplate, was clearly one of discomfort. Quite possibly, he was having second thoughts about remaining in the vessel with the rest of them.

It wasn't too late to amend that decision. They could still recall the *Livingston*. However, Ben Zoma couldn't suggest the idea. It would have to come from McAteer.

And as time went on, it didn't. The admiral just explored the interior of the ship with the rest of them, keeping his feelings to himself—whatever they were.

"I think I've located one of their data nodes," Paris announced after a while. He checked his tricorder again, then used his palmlight to point across the chamber. "It's that way."

"Let's check it out," said Ben Zoma, allowing the ensign to take the lead.

Paris led them to a diamond-shaped projection situated about two meters off the ground. Finding a hinge, the ensign swung open a cover to reveal a configuration of illuminated ovals.

Garner ran her tricorder over it. "It's a data node, all right. And it shouldn't be hard to gain access."

"Just what I wanted to hear," said Ben Zoma.

It only took a couple of minutes for Garner to download the contents of the node. Obviously, the invaders hadn't expected anyone to board their supply vessel, or they would have paid a bit more attention to security.

Of course, the information Garner collected was in an alien language. However, their Starfleet-issue tricorders were equipped to deal with that kind of problem. In fact, translating a written language was a lot easier than translating a spoken one.

Ben Zoma took a quick look at the results. There wasn't much in the way of tactical data, since the supply vessel was only programmed to follow the warships. But there was plenty of valuable information in the areas of propulsion and communications.

Not to mention a complete set of cargo consumption projections. With a little work, they could figure out which containers were slated to be off-loaded next, and by which warship.

"Nice going," said Ben Zoma.

Up until that point, the aliens had known a lot more about Starfleet than Starfleet knew about them. Now the shuttle team was starting to even the score.

Picard entered the observation lounge, which was a good deal bigger than the one on the *Stargazer,* and surveyed the faces of those who turned to look up at him.

His host, a large, red-faced man named Shastakovich, got up and extended a meaty paw. "Glad you could make it, Captain."

"So am I," said Picard.

He had received the invitation to beam over to the *Excalibur* only a little more than an hour ago. However, he had made it his business to attend.

In his message, Shastakovich had opined that the

captains of the assembled ships would work together more efficiently if they got to know each other. And with the fleet divided by Captain Sesballa into wings for easier coordination, Shastakovich had opened his ship to all the captains with whom he would be teamed.

One by one, he introduced Picard to his colleagues, all of whom had preceded him there. Nguyen was a tall, slender woman with long, dark hair. Veracruz was stocky and balding with a neatly trimmed goatee. Krellis, a black and white striped Dedderac, was smaller and even more delicate than others of her species. And Minshaya, an Othetaran, sported a lush white beard that all but concealed the copper of his skin.

"Picard . . ." said Veracruz, looking as if he were sampling an exotic taste for the first time.

"Yes," said the captain, his back straightening at the unexpected attention. "Why do you ask?"

"Well," said Veracruz, his gaze hardening as he leaned forward in his seat, "I've heard a great deal about you. For instance, that you're too young and inexperienced to command a starship."

It had the tone of a challenge. Picard had no choice but to respond in kind.

"People say lots of things, Captain. And others, who should know better, repeat them."

Veracruz stared at him for a moment, his mouth a thin, hard line. Then he grinned and jerked a thumb in Picard's direction. "I like this one," he said.

Grinning even wider, Shastakovich clapped Picard on the shoulder. "So do I."

Picard was openmouthed. "But . . ."

"But you were wondering if we would treat you like an equal," said Nguyen, a knowing smile spreading across her face. "Tell the truth now."

"I . . . suppose I was," Picard admitted.

"We've all heard good things about you," said Krellis, her dark eyes gleaming. "That was why we were pleased when Sesballa assigned us to the same wing."

"Good things," said Picard, scarcely able to believe it.

"I know," said Minshaya, his voice deep and sonorous. "You have been browbeaten so badly by Admiral McAteer, you have come to question your worth."

"Before we go any further," said Shastakovich, his bushy brows meeting over his nose, "we should establish something. What's said in this room stays in this room—no exceptions. Agreed?"

"Of course," said Picard. "My lips are sealed."

"Then I can tell you this about Admiral McAteer," said Veracruz. "He doesn't like *any* of us very much. If he had his way, he'd ship us all off to desk jobs somewhere."

"Except Greenbriar and Sesballa," said Nguyen, "and a handful of his other favorites. He'd keep them around to set an example."

Picard was comforted to learn that. "And here I thought I was his only whipping boy."

"Not the *only* one," said Nguyen. "Just his favorite. He can't seem to get past your age."

Shastakovich snorted. "Maybe it makes him feel inadequate by comparison. He's very proud of how rapidly he became an admiral, you know."

It had never occurred to Picard that McAteer might be jealous of him. Obviously, his fellow captains had analyzed the admiral a good deal more thoroughly than he had.

"Don't let it bother you," said Krellis. "Eventually, he'll get used to your being around."

"You were given your command by Admiral Mehdi," said Veracruz. "McAteer knows he's not supposed to mess with another admiral's appointments."

"Actually," Picard said soberly, "he has done that already. He scheduled a competency hearing for me back on Earth."

The other captains stared at him in disbelief. The only sound in the room was the muted hum of the engines.

"You are joking," Minshaya said at last.

"I wish I were," said Picard.

Nguyen shook her head. "That's outrageous."

Shastakovich made a sound of disgust in his throat. "Don't worry. You'll beat him."

Picard wished he were half as certain as his colleague. "Thank you for saying so."

The others expressed the same sort of sentiment as Shastakovich. However, Picard could see in their eyes that they were just being supportive. They knew the kind of trap he was in, and how slim the odds were of escaping it.

"In any case," said Minshaya, "we did not come

here to talk about our friend Picard. We came to discuss strategy."

"Indeed," said Shastakovich. "Let's get to work.
Judging from the reports, this will not be easy."

Suddenly, they were all business. Picard took a seat
and endeavored to adopt the same attitude.

"How do you work a battle?" asked Veracruz,
throwing the question out to the entire group. "Do you
like to take the offensive? Or do you prefer to hang
back and let the enemy come to you?"

Shastakovich turned to Picard. "Why don't we start
over here and work our way around the room?"

Picard nodded and said, "Well, it depends . . ."

Kastiigan sat down at his desk in the sciences
section and went over the report from the *Exeter,*
which the captain had made available to all his
section heads. It was basically a list of newly arrived
vessels.

The *Hood,* commanded by Captain Benderrek. The
Valdemar, commanded by Captain Calabrese. And the
Etrechaya, which had been commissioned only a cou-
ple of days earlier.

That made thirty-two vessels in all. It was already
one of the most powerful forces in Starfleet history,
and still more ships were on the way.

But then, the invaders were powerful too. Otherwise,
they couldn't have taken those other ships so easily.

Kastiigan sat back in his chair. There would be no
negotiating with this enemy—he had heard his crewmates agree on that time and again. The invaders were

too vicious, too implacable, too *alien.* The only way to stop them was to overcome them.

Combat, the science officer thought. Just the prospect of it made his heart beat a little faster. It was what he had hoped for when he signed on with the *Stargazer* months earlier. It was what he had dreamed about.

Since Kastiigan's arrival on board, Captain Picard had put his life on the line several times. So had a number of his officers. But never Kastiigan. Not even *once.*

He had expressed his desire to do so on more than one occasion. He had started out subtly and grown increasingly blunt. And yet, his requests had fallen on deaf ears.

Over and over again, he had watched others assume the risks that should have been his. And with each oversight, his disappointment had gotten a little keener.

It had gotten to the point where Kastiigan was resigned to his fate. He had given up hoping that he would ever have the opportunity he longed for.

Now, with a clash of such huge proportions imminent, his hopes were rekindled. Finally, he stood a chance of seizing the glory that had so far eluded him.

And it might not be at the captain's behest. In battle, one never knew when the need for sacrifice might arise—a situation where a single death might prevent a great many others.

If it comes, Kastiigan thought, *I'll be ready.* The way his stint on the *Stargazer* had gone, he couldn't depend on getting a second chance. He just had to make sure he didn't waste the first one.

Ben Zoma stopped and regarded the collection of containers in front of him, using his palmlight for illumination.

"And they're the next ones to go?" he asked.

"They're *among* the next ones," said Garner. "But we won't be able to fit inside any of the others."

There would be plenty of room for them to fit inside the gigantic specimens before him. There were nearly a dozen of the dark, cylindrical behemoths, each one almost as large as the *Livingston*. And the aliens had started out with even more of them, judging by the circular dust-marks left on the floor.

Of course, Ben Zoma and his team needed only one of the containers. As big as the things were, there would be more than enough room inside for all of them.

But which one would the aliens grab first? The shuttle team's best bet seemed to be the container closest to the cargo bay door, which wasn't more than a hundred meters away—but they couldn't be certain of it. And the longer it took them to smuggle themselves aboard a warship, the more punishment Starfleet would be forced to endure.

"Just one problem," said Horombo, using his palmlight to inspect one of the containers. "They're locked."

Indeed, the container had four clasps positioned at regular intervals around its lid. They were each about the size of Ben Zoma's fist, with a small, horizontal readout and a keypad.

"That shouldn't be a problem," said McAteer, uttering his first words since they entered the supply drone.

"Not in terms of getting in," said Ben Zoma, choosing his words carefully so as not to make the admiral look bad. "But after we're inside, we'll have to reactivate the locks."

"Of course," said McAteer, as if he had already considered that aspect of the situation.

"I think we'll be all right," said Horombo, scanning the locking mechanisms with his tricorder. "They don't look all that complicated."

McAteer seemed pleased with the observation. "Didn't expect they would be."

It was Chen who finally cracked the code and opened the locks. They opened slowly, with a whirring sound.

Climbing up on Ben Zoma's back, Garner lifted the container's lid and used her palmlight to take a look inside.

"What's in there?" Ramirez asked, her face cast into stark relief by the play of light beams.

"Rolls of something," said Garner. "Registers organic." She whistled. "A fair amount of bacteria here. Hard to say if it's harmful or not."

It wasn't the *best* news. Their suits afforded them their own air supplies, but only for a limited amount of time. And when they arrived on the alien warship, they would want to sacrifice protection for freedom of movement anyway.

As Garner climbed down, she said, "A bit of a problem."

But there was a solution. "Let's get that stuff out of the container," said Ben Zoma, "and put it somewhere else. Then we'll cleanse the inside of the container with our phasers."

"We'll need to record its mass," said Chen, "so we know how much to add to our own."

It was a good point. They didn't want to give the aliens any reason to question what they were bringing aboard.

"That'll be your job," Ben Zoma told him.

"Maybe we should keep a *little* of the stuff," said Paris, "to line the inside of the container—in case they run a scan."

Another good point. But then, they were back to square one with regard to the bacteria. *Or maybe not. . . .*

"Let's try this," said Ben Zoma. He indicated the container's immediate neighbors with a sweep of his hand. "Check these other monsters for bacteria. If they're germ-free, we can transplant some of their contents into this one."

"Sounds good," said McAteer, apparently feeling he had to say *something.*

As it turned out, the next container they opened was free of the bacteria. Luck, it seemed, was still on their side.

Ben Zoma assigned three of the security officers—Horombo, Ramirez, and Garner—to empty out the first container. Then he, Paris, and Chen undertook to empty the second one.

The cargo they handled was pale, flat, and flexible.

It was packed in rolls as Garner had indicated, each of them half a head taller than Ben Zoma and probably just as heavy. Being organic, it seemed likely that it was a foodstuff of some kind.

McAteer, to his credit, didn't stand around and watch everyone else work. Joining the first team, he pitched in and worked as hard as anyone.

Little by little, they created two stacks a good forty meters apart from each other, to minimize the possibility of cross-contamination. Then Ben Zoma's team went to work on the first container, scouring it with wide-angle phaser beams.

When their tricorders stopped registering bacteria, they began filling the container with germ-free cargo, using approximately half the stack they made—enough to reach the mass level that had existed in the container before.

Meanwhile, the first team filled the second container with the stack of bacteria-infested cargo. By the time they finished and were ready to lock the lid down, Ben Zoma's team was distributing the excess from the germ-free pile to the other containers—not just the second one, but also those that were previously unopened.

That way, they could hide the cargo they were displacing. And unless the aliens scrutinized the contents of each container, they would never know what had happened.

After Ben Zoma and his team finished, they took out their phasers again and used the same low-level, wide-angle setting they had used on the container to burn germs off each other. Otherwise, they might have contaminated the bacteria-free cargo and undone all their hard work.

The only thing left to do was figure out how to reset the locks after they climbed into the container. While Chen and Garner worked on that, Ben Zoma told the rest of his team to take a break.

He had intended to take one himself. However, as he watched Chen and Garner work on the problem, he heard McAteer's voice in the confines of his helmet.

"Can I speak with you for a moment?" the admiral asked. He tapped his helmet with a gloved forefinger. "Without these?"

Ben Zoma understood the implication. As it was, they could speak over the group com link or by putting their helmets together. But neither way afforded them any real privacy.

"Of course," said the first officer.

He cast his palmlight about until he found a likely collection of containers. After all, there was more to privacy than keeping their choice of words to themselves.

He tilted his head. "Over there would be good."

McAteer nodded. "Fine with me, Commander." Then he led the way, forcing Ben Zoma to follow.

When they reached the far side of the cluster, the admiral took off his helmet, and Ben Zoma did the same. As their tricorders had indicated, the air was warm and breathable.

"What was it you wanted to talk about?" Ben Zoma asked, getting straight to the point.

"You," said McAteer. "And the way you've conducted yourself since we entered this ship."

The first officer wasn't sure what he had expected to hear, but it wasn't *that.* "I'm not sure what you mean, sir."

"You've been giving orders as if I weren't around. As if I weren't the ranking officer on this mission."

"With all due respect, Admiral, I thought you were happy to let me take the lead. You certainly didn't give me any indication to the contrary."

"Well," said McAteer, "I'm giving you an indication now. I'm the one who'll be giving the orders from now on. And if you have a problem with that, you'll have to cope with it."

Ben Zoma felt as if he had been slapped in the face. Still, he managed to keep his composure. "I have no problem with it, sir."

The admiral chuckled derisively. "Really, Commander? You bear me no ill at all?"

The first officer saw now what McAteer was getting at. But just because the admiral was dangling the bait, he didn't have to rise to it. "None at all, sir."

McAteer scowled. "Come on, Commander, you can say it. You don't like the fact that I've called your captain to a competence hearing."

Ben Zoma shrugged. "Why wouldn't I like that?"

"Because he's your friend, for one thing. And because if he's demoted, there's a good chance his first officer will be knocked down as well."

Obviously, Ben Zoma had considered that possibility. But truthfully, he didn't want to serve under anyone except Picard. If his friend were stripped of his command, Ben Zoma would be happy to leave with him.

"I suppose you think you have good cause to call for a hearing," said the first officer. "Well, I don't."

"Really," said the admiral. "I'd like to hear more."

"Permission to speak freely?"

"Granted," said McAteer.

"From where I stand, Captain Picard has done pretty much everything you've asked of him. If he's been deficient at all, it's in his reluctance to tell you where to get off."

McAteer's face suffused with blood. "I've bent over backward to be fair to your captain, Commander. Despite his inexperience, I've treated him like any other captain in my sector."

"You've given him two kinds of missions, Admiral—the kind in which he can't possibly succeed and the kind that pushes him out of the way. Don't tell me you call that being fair."

"I *wanted* to trust him," said McAteer. "But after the mess he made of his contact with the Nuyyad, what was I supposed to do? Give him another chance to screw things up?"

Ben Zoma met his gaze. "Picard handled the Nuyyad the way any good captain would have handled them. They were out for our blood from the moment we laid eyes on them. If you had been there, you would have seen that."

"If the Nuyyad were out for blood, it was because you were in their space."

"We were in their space," said the first officer, "because they lured us there."

"If I recall correctly," said McAteer, "it was your friend *Santana* who lured you there."

"Under orders from the Nuyyad."

"You didn't know that at the time."

"We were attacked," said Ben Zoma. "We defended ourselves."

"And went on defending yourself, even when you had to look high and low for someone to defend yourselves *against.*"

"What should we have done?" Ben Zoma asked. "Abandoned a colony full of human beings?"

"You should have done your *job,*" said McAteer, "which, if I recall correctly, was simply to reconnoiter and report to Starfleet Command."

"Is that all you expect of your captains? Reconnaissance? Even when there's a clearcut danger to the Federation, and it's in their power to eliminate it?"

"Clearcut to *whom,* Commander?"

"To the man who was *there,* Admiral. Certainly clear to *him,* and to anyone who was fighting alongside him."

"Then," said McAteer, "I question *all* your judgments."

Ben Zoma laughed. "Why not? It's a lot easier than questioning your own."

The admiral gave him a hard look. "My judgment is based on decades of experience."

"So is Admiral Mehdi's," said Ben Zoma, "and he's

given Captain Picard a vote of confidence. Why can't you?"

"Why?" The admiral snorted. "Because it's not my job to make someone else's bad decisions look good. Making Picard a captain was a bad decision."

"Nothing like keeping an open mind."

"Open minds," McAteer snapped, "are for people who lack conviction."

Ben Zoma stared at him. How could he argue with someone who believed that?

"In any case," said McAteer, "this is the wrong time and place to debate the wisdom of your captain's decisions. If you want to defend him, you can do it when his case is heard."

"I will," said Ben Zoma, putting his helmet back on.

If we live that long, he added silently.

Chapter Thirteen

PICARD SWORE BENEATH HIS BREATH as he read the information on Paxton's monitor screen.

Two more starships had dropped off the subspace communications map. One was the *Yorenda,* whose Vulcan first officer had graduated from the Academy just ahead of Picard. The other was the *Gettysburg,* commanded by Tabitha Jenkins, ahead of even Sesbella in terms of longevity.

Neither vessel had been much farther out from Earth than the *Stargazer* when Command lost contact with them. If the aliens were responsible for the disappearances, they were a good deal closer than anyone had expected.

Close enough to clash with Starfleet's line of defense sometime in the next few hours. It was a daunting thought.

And it had to be even more daunting to the rank and file, Picard reflected. No one knew that better than he, who had been one of them until a few short months ago.

He looked around his bridge, noting the air of tension that pervaded the place. Expressions were strained, shoulder muscles taut, postures painfully erect.

Not one of his officers was taking the enemy lightly. Nor could they. Not with the stakes so terribly high.

The captain wished he could say something to lift everyone's spirits. Had Ben Zoma been there, he would have found a way—perhaps with a word, perhaps with just a gesture.

But Picard didn't have his first officer's knack in that regard. All he could do was move from station to station and let his people know they weren't alone.

"Thank you," he told Paxton.

"No problem, sir."

Picard regarded the com officer. "How are you holding up, Lieutenant?"

Paxton smiled in his full, dark beard. "Well enough. I just can't help thinking . . ." He shrugged.

"What?" said the captain.

"That I could possibly have prevented this. If I'd caught Ulelo before he sent out those specs, the invaders wouldn't have gained an advantage over us."

"None of us noticed what Ulelo was up to," said Picard. "You, at least, have an excuse—you were absent from the bridge when he was transmitting his data. I was here almost all the time, just a few meters away from him." He looked around. "So were Idun and Gerda, and Commander Ben Zoma, and Commander Wu."

Paxton sighed. "Yes, but if I'd checked the com logs a little sooner, I would have seen that something was wrong."

Picard dismissed the idea with a wave of his hand. "It is to your credit that you checked them *at all*. As you know, most com officers do not bother—and if I had had one of them instead of you, Ulelo would still be sending out his messages undetected and unimpeded."

That seemed to make Paxton feel better about himself. "Well," he said, "when you put it that way . . ."

Picard clapped him on the shoulder. "Forget about Ulelo. Just keep the lines of communication open during the battle, and you will have done all I can possibly expect of you."

Paxton nodded. "Thanks, sir."

"For what?" Picard asked with a wink. Then he moved aft to see to Urajel, who had been chosen to man the engineering station in the event of a battle.

He would ask her how she was doing, and try to answer any concerns she might have, and let her know that he had faith in her—just as he had done with Paxton. It wouldn't accomplish much—the captain knew that. But it would be better than nothing.

As Horombo had predicted, it didn't take long for Ben Zoma's team to devise a way to relock the container lid.

In the end, they opted to phaser holes in the wall of the container from the inside. By continuing through the back of each lock, they obtained access to its insides and were able to reconfigure it to accept a tricorder signal.

After that, it was a matter of climbing inside. That was accomplished with the help of a couple of strong backs, Ben Zoma's being one of them.

Garner was the last to clear the wall of the container. Having been a gymnast of some note, she was able to take a running jump and vault over it, though her form was hampered considerably by the bulkiness of her containment suit.

The next step was to drag the lid across the top of the container until it slipped into place, and then to reactivate the locks. They were already depending on their palmlights for illumination, so it didn't get any darker when they pulled the lid over. But somehow, it *seemed* like it did.

And their lights had limited power sources. In a little while they would have to be turned off, so the team could make use of them again when they really needed them.

It wouldn't be a bad idea to conserve air as well. They didn't know what conditions they might face in transit from the supply drone to a warship. In fact, the sooner they made the move, the better.

"Remove your helmets," Ben Zoma ordered his companions, "and shut down your air intake."

No one hesitated—except McAteer. The admiral tossed him a look that said *he* would have liked to give that order.

The first officer had agreed to defer to McAteer, but he wasn't going to ask permission every time he saw a need to say something. And if the admiral didn't like it, he could convene a competency hearing for Ben Zoma as well.

He was still thinking that when something unpleasant reached his nostrils. Something *very* unpleasant. And he didn't have to look far to realize what it was.

McAteer uttered a sound of disgust. "It stinks in here!"

"So it does," said Ben Zoma. He pointed to the foodstuff with which they had lined the container. "And here's the culprit."

Ramirez took a whiff of it close up, then made a face. "The commander's right."

The admiral turned to Ben Zoma as if the first officer had created the smell himself. "What are we going to do about it?"

Ben Zoma shrugged. "Not much we *can* do, sir. We could put the stuff somewhere else, but if the aliens shallow-scan the container they won't find what they're looking for."

The admiral looked like he was on the verge of supporting that option, even with its obvious drawback. Then he seemed to feel the scrutiny of the away team.

"Very well," he said, his eyes narrowing. "We'll do it your way, Mister Ben Zoma."

The first officer met McAteer's glare. "Make yourselves at home, then. We'll be here awhile."

A few hours, in fact. At least, that was what the aliens' pickup schedule had indicated.

It might have been more comfortable for everyone if they propped their backs up against the walls of the container. However, no one wanted to get closer to the foodstuff than was absolutely necessary, so they all clustered in the middle.

Then they waited, thinking their own private thoughts, their features sculpted by the glow of Chen's lonely palmlight. And soon, they would have to give that up as well.

Ben Zoma felt as if he had climbed a beanstalk to a colossal castle and was waiting in a cheese larder for the giant to come home. Of course, he couldn't imagine any cheese larder smelling as bad as the stuff around him.

But considering the magnitude of what was at stake, he would have endured a lot worse.

Picard had no sooner emerged from his ready room onto the *Stargazer*'s bridge than he was called over by Gerda Asmund.

"What is it?" he asked, joining her at her console.

She pointed. "I think you should take a look at this, sir."

The screen the navigator showed him was black with red dots on it, tracking the aliens' progress through the sector. The captain didn't have to study it for long to understand why Gerda found it intriguing.

"You see what I mean?" she asked.

Picard nodded. "I do."

The armada had come within a light-year of several different Federation member worlds, all of them blessed with abundant populations and natural resources. But the aliens hadn't seen fit to attack them—hadn't even slowed down to get a better look at what they were passing up.

For no reason Picard could fathom, the invaders were interested only in the *Stargazer* and her sister ships—even though they had already caught and released half a dozen of them. It was bizarre—beyond bizarre. And yet, there it was, a pattern that was documented and undeniable.

The captain glanced at Gerda. "I don't suppose you would care to venture an explanation."

She shook her head. "Not without more to go on."

Picard grunted. "That makes two of us."

Still puzzling over what he had seen, he deposited himself in his center seat and regarded his viewscreen. There was nothing remarkable on it at the moment. But in time, there would be.

Their mysterious enemy would fill it with its armada, cutting like a dagger through Federation space. And it would be up to Picard and others like him to turn the dagger away.

He would have accepted the challenge more eagerly if he thought he and his fellow captains had an even chance. But this was one battle he didn't think they could win.

Four hours had passed in the container, and the aliens still hadn't come for it. What's more, the smell inside it hadn't gotten any better.

Ben Zoma decided his team needed a distraction. Certainly, he did.

"So," he said, "who's got an Academy story?"

At first, everyone just stared at him. Then Horombo chuckled to himself and said, "I do, I guess."

"Let's hear it," said Ben Zoma.

McAteer looked at him as if he disapproved of the idea. However, he didn't actually come out and put the kibosh on it.

"Well," said Horombo, "you all know Boothby, right?"

There was a murmur of confirmation. Boothby was the groundskeeper at the Academy, a very popular figure with the cadets.

But not with McAteer, apparently. He had a queer look in his eye, as if the mention of Boothby brought back a memory he would rather have forgotten.

"About ten years back," said Horombo, "when I was attending the Academy, Boothby planted a Vulcan *tuula* bush. It was dark red, with slim, pointed leaves."

"I remember it," said Paris, and apparently he wasn't the only one there who did.

"Anyway," Horombo continued, "one record-cold night, a few of the other cadets got their hands on some pretty strong liquor—not Romulan ale, but something almost as potent—elsewhere in San Francisco. Two bottles altogether. By the time they got back to the Academy grounds, they had already finished one of the bottles and were half-blind.

"They figured they would sock away the other bottle for another day. But as they crossed Boothby's gardens to get to their dorm rooms, they saw a security officer strolling in their direction. Afraid that he would ask to see what they were carrying, they panicked and slipped behind the *tuula* bush, and poured out the contents of the second bottle.

"As it turned out, the security officer took a different route and didn't bother them, so they had emptied the bottle for nothing. But that wasn't the worst of it. The next day, when they walked past the tuula bush, it wasn't dark red anymore. Its leaves were all pink with brown spots.

"Well, all the cadets loved Boothby, and these three were no exception. They knew how hard he had worked to nurture his *tuula* bush, and how heartbroken he would be to see what they had done to it. And they knew also how angry the commandant of the Academy would be if he found out how the *tuula* bush had gotten sick.

"In the end, they decided to do the honorable thing and admit their mistake, regardless of the trouble they would face. But first, they went to Boothby to apologize—and it was a good thing they did.

"Apparently, *tuula* bushes change colors with the seasons, and this one got confused by the drastic change in temperature that evening. So it faded from its summer scarlet to its colder-weather pink and brown in just a couple of hours—and had already made the change when the cadets came along and dumped liquor on it."

"So it wasn't their fault," said Ramirez, a smile on her face.

"Not at all. In fact, the bush had already changed back to its summer coloring. And Boothby being Boothby, he didn't tell anyone what the cadets had done."

Ben Zoma laughed. "Good story, Lieutenant."

Everyone else seemed to think so, too. Except McAteer, of course. But then, he was the odd man out more and more.

"And this was ten years ago?" asked Garner.

Horombo nodded. "My senior year. Were you there?"

Garner shook her head. "Not yet. I got there the year after—when Oonnoommi took over as commandant."

Ramirez leaned forward. "Wasn't that the year the Parisses Squares team went undefeated?"

"That was the year before," said Chen. "My brother—" He stopped in midsentence, his eyes suddenly wide and desolate.

"Your brother *what?*" asked Ben Zoma, refusing to let the security officer wallow in uncertainty.

"My brother," Chen said a little more quietly, "was on that team."

"And how did he do?" the first officer asked.

Chen smiled despite himself. "He did well, sir. As a matter of fact, he led the cadets in scoring."

"Glad to hear it," said Ben Zoma.

"That's it," McAteer said abruptly.

Ben Zoma turned to him. "Sir?"

"I'm tired of waiting," the admiral said. "While we're sitting here twiddling our damn thumbs, the aliens may be mopping the floor with our fleet."

It was a possibility, all right. But Ben Zoma wasn't inclined to act on it.

"We've got to be patient," he said.

"Patience hasn't gotten us anywhere," the admiral noted. "We've got to expedite the process somehow."

The first officer regarded McAteer. "There's no need. The aliens might not always stick to their replenishment schedule, but they'll be by soon enough."

The admiral scowled. "Soon enough for *you,* maybe. But I don't intend to stay here in this can for the—"

Suddenly, a *clang* went through the deckplates. It sounded as if the supply carrier had struck something.

Or maybe *docked* with something.

Ben Zoma hoped like crazy that it was the latter possibility. Otherwise, he would have to listen to McAteer that much longer.

"Turn off the light," he said, "and put on your helmets. I've got a feeling this is our ride."

Chapter Fourteen

THE CONTAINER'S TRANSIT from the supply drone to what was presumably a warship was quick and smooth. Unless Ben Zoma missed his guess, it was made possible by some kind of tractor beam, which lifted them off the drone's deck and put them down again a few minutes later.

According to Chen's tricorder, the temperature in the container dropped precipitously for those few minutes, but it was climbing again just as steeply now. That meant the hold they occupied was heated, just like the drone.

Chen whispered that there was air there too—no great surprise. But it allowed them to divest themselves of their suits, which restricted movement, and they would need all the movement they could get.

Then came the big question. "Any guards out there?" asked Ben Zoma.

"We're alone," said Chen, his face caught in the glow of his tricorder readout.

That was the best news of all.

Their next step was to locate a data node—a task Ramirez had been assigned while they were still on the drone. Fortunately, they had accessed one on the supply ship and knew what to look for.

At the same time, Garner set about finding something resembling a shuttlebay. Ben Zoma's plan was to split the team into two groups. One would hunt down the node, download the data, and transmit it across the ship tricorder-to-tricorder. The other group would secure a shuttle—if the warship even had one—receive the data, and retransmit it using the craft's com system. They would hold the shuttle until the other group rejoined them.

Of course, the first officer knew that escape was a long shot. Their main priority was just to get the data off to Starfleet.

Unfortunately, Ramirez had only been searching for a few seconds before Ben Zoma's plan hit a snag. He could tell by the security officer's expression.

"What's wrong?" he said.

Ramirez frowned. "Something in the bulkheads is blocking the signal. I think I can find a node, but we're not going to be able to transmit intraship."

"We've got a shuttlebay," Garner announced, "or something like it. Three decks down." She swore under her breath. "I just can't tell if it's guarded or not, thanks to that problem with the bulkheads."

"All right," said Ramirez, "I found a node. One deck up."

"We can use the lift system," Paris chimed in. His assignment had been to figure out how the invaders got around their vessel, since the drone was all on one level and didn't need such a thing. "It's a little like ours," he said, "but it only moves up and down. No horizontal routes."

"What's the best lift for us to take?" Ben Zoma asked.

Paris studied his tricorder screen. "After we leave this room, it's down the corridor to the right. About fifty meters."

Ben Zoma absorbed the information. "All right. We'll do this the hard way." He took in the rest of the team at a glance. "We'll download the data and carry it to the shuttlebay. And we'll all go together, to minimize the chances of our being discovered."

No one objected—not even McAteer. All he said was, "What are we waiting for? Let's spring the locks."

For once, Ben Zoma agreed with him. Turning to Horombo, whom he knew was beside him, he said, "No time like the present."

"Aye, sir," said Horombo.

Activating his palmlight, he gave them something to see by. Then the other security officers used their tricorders to open the locks one at a time.

That done, they slid the lid partway off the container. It gave them access to ambient light, allowing Horombo to douse his palm device.

With help from Paris, Ben Zoma peeked over the edge of the container wall. He saw the same serpentine motifs they had encountered in the supply drone, but they covered a much smaller space—perhaps five times the size of the *Livingston*.

At the moment, theirs was the only container in the enclosure. That supported a theory Paris had put forth that the aliens destroyed each container when they were done with it. After all, there weren't any empties on the drone, and the warships didn't have a lot of room for them.

Ben Zoma pulled himself over the top of the wall and lowered himself to the deck. Then he drew his phaser and whispered for the others to follow.

After they were all out, they pushed the lid back into place and reset the locks. That way if an alien entered the bay, he wouldn't think anything was amiss. To discover that, he would have to open the container.

But the aliens might not do that for some time. And by then it would already be obvious that someone had slipped aboard the warship—because the team had either escaped or been killed for their trespass.

"Remember what we talked about," said Ben Zoma. "We move quickly and quietly. And we stay alert."

They all nodded by way of acknowledgment. All except McAteer. Asserting his rank, he said, "Let's go."

As the admiral moved off, Ben Zoma gestured for Chen to stay close to him. After all, *someone* had to.

They didn't find any door controls at the cargo bay's exit. But then, they didn't need any. The doors opened automatically, giving them access to the corridor.

It was narrow and dimly lit. In accordance with Paris's instructions, they went right, their phasers at the ready. But they didn't run into any opposition.

When they reached the lift it opened for them, just as the doors to the bay had. After they piled into the narrow compartment, barely fitting their entire team, there was a tense moment when it seemed the door might not close.

But eventually, it did. And a few moments later, it opened again, giving them access to the floor above. Again, the corridor was empty. Ben Zoma thanked whatever fate had seen fit to smile on them and led the way to the node.

It looked exactly like the one they had accessed on the drone. In a matter of seconds, Horombo had it open and had begun the downloading process.

They all listened for approaching footsteps. But there weren't any. At least, for the time being.

Above all else, Picard hated waiting. And yet, he had done more of that than anything else in the last couple of days.

At the moment, he was doing his waiting in his ready room. He was going over reports from helm, weapons, engineering, security, even medical—assurances that everyone would be ready when the battle got under way. And that would have been fine, except he had gone over the reports twice already.

There was simply nothing left to do. Nothing but watch the stars and wait for the enemy to emerge from among them.

The captain was pleased when he heard the chime that told him someone wanted a word with him. If nothing else, it would serve as a break in the monotony.

"Come," he said.

It was Wu. And judging from the vaguely troubled look on her face, she had just come from another visit with Lieutenant Ulelo.

"Anything new?" Picard asked.

"Nothing," she replied. "Unfortunately. All I'm doing is making him more agitated with all my questions."

"Perhaps you should let up for a while."

"Perhaps," she allowed. "Or perhaps I should push even harder. I just don't know."

It wasn't often that Wu allowed herself to express uncertainty. The fact that she had chosen to do so now was a measure of how very difficult her assignment was.

But the captain couldn't imagine giving it to anyone else. "You will figure it out," he said. "I know you will."

The second officer smiled. "I appreciate the vote of confidence."

"It is well founded," Picard assured her.

At least she didn't have to go over reports for the third time. Of everyone on the *Stargazer*, Wu was the only one who still had an unfinished assignment.

He almost envied her.

Ben Zoma and his team had been downloading information from the aliens' data node for almost three minutes when McAteer clapped Garner on the shoulder.

"Let's go," he said.

"I'm not finished," the security officer told him.

"Yes, you are," said McAteer.

"But, sir—" Garner started.

The admiral raised a hand to cut her off. "I don't

185

think it's wise to push our luck, Lieutenant. We need to get out of here before we're discovered."

Garner obviously disagreed, but it wasn't her place to say so. Instead, she looked to Ben Zoma.

"There's a lot more data to be gathered," the first officer pointed out, keeping his tone reasonable so as not to antagonize McAteer. "We're only going to get one shot at this. We may as well get everything we can."

The admiral stared at him. For a moment, Ben Zoma was certain that McAteer was going to put his foot down. Then something seemed to soften in him.

"All right," he said, "have it your way, Commander. We'll keep going for a while."

Ben Zoma nodded. "Thank you, sir."

He woke up in the heavy, pulsating darkness, his skin clammy, his heart pounding. Before he knew it, he was sitting bolt upright, waiting for awareness to come.

But it didn't. There was only the starless night, always and forever. He couldn't remember a time when it wasn't there, when he knew something hard and real to hang on to.

And who was he, in that stark, black night? What was his name, his parentage, his place in the universe?

He didn't know—either who he was or what he was doing there. He didn't know *anything*.

I am someone, he insisted. *I have a name, a body, a face. I come from somewhere.*

All he had to do was dredge it out of the depths, drag out the answers that would create his world piece by piece. All he had to do was *remember.*

Slowly, ever so slowly, the darkness relented. Things took on shape and substance around him. The bed he was sitting in, drenching the covers with his sweat. A chair. A set of clothes draped over the back of it.

And outside, someone. A person, like himself. A female. As he watched, she turned to him.

"Lieutenant?" she said.

Her tone was one of concern. But more than that was what she had said. *Lieutenant.* He was a *lieutenant.*

Yes . . . on a ship. With other crewmen, a great many of them. He could see them in his mind's eye, walking the corridors, dressed in red and black uniforms.

Then it came to him—what he was, where he was. Who he was. *My name is Ulelo,* he told himself. *Dikembe Ulelo. I'm a communications officer on the* Stargazer.

But no . . . he was more than that, wasn't he? He was a plant, a spy who had come to the *Stargazer* to transmit information about the ship to his comrades.

And who were they, again? He couldn't remember. It was insane. He had sent out that information at great risk to himself. Whom had he done it for?

And *why?* For the love of reason, *why?*

Ulelo had no answer—though he had a feeling he had posed the question before. It was as if there were a great, dark abyss at his feet, an echoing, bottomless gulf that swallowed everything he needed to know.

Suddenly, he saw it—the abyss, as if it had always been there. It was immense, a universe unto itself. He could feel the chill rising from it, smell its fetid breath.

And it wasn't just his memories that it craved, sucking them down into its depths with infinite hunger. It was Ulelo himself—because without his memories he was nothing . . .

Nothing at all.

He felt empty in the presence of all that darkness, so empty. There was no substance to him, no weight, nothing to keep him anchored to the ground. And the abyss was so hungry, so insistent on having him.

Ulelo didn't want to be drawn in, but he had no strength to stop himself. He could feel himself falling, twisting in a decay-breath of wind, surrounded by it, engulfed by it. . . .

No! he screamed, frantic to get back to the brink where he had stood. But it was soaring up and away from him, more impossible to reach with every breathless second.

No! he shrieked, his cries consumed by the rush of darkness all around him. *Nooo . . . !*

Chapter Fifteen

GREYHORSE DARTED INTO THE BRIG, a med pack slung over his shoulder. At the end of the short hall where Ulelo's cell was situated, the electromagnetic barrier was down, and Joseph and Pierzynski were attending to the prisoner.

"What happened?" asked the doctor as he forcibly moved Pierzynski out of the way.

"He just started yelling," said Joseph, who stood back of his own volition. "No warning or anything. Then *this.*"

Ulelo was twitching, his eyes had rolled back into their sockets, and his tongue was lolling uncontrollably in his mouth. It was clearly a seizure of some kind.

Scanning Ulelo with his tricorder, Greyhorse consulted its readout. It was a seizure, all right, and a serious one at that. Ulelo needed to be sedated before he swallowed his tongue or otherwise injured himself.

Pulling a hypospray out of his pack, Greyhorse punched in a formula and held the device against Ulelo's neck. Then he released the hypospray's content into his patient's carotid artery.

The medication shouldn't have taken more than a moment to start working. But after three or four seconds, the doctor didn't notice any effect.

Some people were more resistant to certain drugs than others, but Greyhorse had called for a rather large dose. Frowning, he programmed a different formula into the hypospray and applied it again to Ulelo's neck.

This time, it had the desired effect. The twitching stopped and Ulelo slumped peacefully in the doctor's arms.

Joseph breathed a sigh of relief. "I don't remember seeing anything about seizures in Ulelo's file."

"That's because there was nothing there," said Greyhorse. "He had no record of seizures." *Until now.*

"Will he be okay here in the brig?" Joseph asked.

The doctor shook his head. "I wouldn't chance it. He'll have to be moved to sickbay."

"That'll require the captain's authorization," said Pierzynski.

Greyhorse shot a look at him. "Then get it."

Nikolas had spent his fair share of time in the *Stargazer*'s Jefferies tubes, and never thought much of the experience. But then, he hadn't seen the access tubes in the *Iktoj'ni.*

"You know," he told Locklear as they descended a

ladder built into the side of the tube, "it's a good thing I didn't have a big lunch. Otherwise, I might not fit."

"I thought you Starfleet types never complained," said Locklear.

"Who's complaining? I'm just making an observation."

"Just four or five more rungs," said Locklear, who was leading the way down. "I can see the problem from here."

They had been sent to repair a break in the internal sensor network—something that just never happened on a starship. But then, vessels like the *Stargazer* used new parts, not whatever the captain could get a deal on.

"Okay," said Locklear, "I'm there. Pass the—"

"Don't tell me," said Nikolas, "I know." He had become as conversant with the *Iktoj'ni*'s tool kits as anyone in the time he had spent on board.

Taking the leathery black bag off his shoulder, he pulled it open and selected the required device. Then he handed it down to his friend.

"Thanks," said Locklear.

"Hey," said Nikolas, "don't mention it."

"You know," said Locklear, working on the sensor break, "you never told me what made you decide to leave Starfleet."

"Didn't I?" said Nikolas.

"Nope. But I've got my suspicions."

"Do tell."

"It was a girl, wasn't it? It's always a girl."

Nikolas didn't deny it.

"You met her on the *Stargazer?*"

Nikolas sighed—giving his friend all the answer he needed.

"What happened to her?"

"She disappeared." It was no more than the truth.

Locklear looked up at him. "She got a transfer?"

"I suppose you could say that."

Suddenly, Nikolas felt the ladder jerk beneath his feet. It was a disconcerting feeling, to say the least. Unfortunately, it wasn't an unfamiliar one. He recalled it all too vividly from the time he spent in Starfleet.

"What was that?" Locklear asked.

Before he got all the words out, Nikolas felt a second jolt. And then a third.

"We're under attack," he said.

"You sure?" asked Locklear, who as a merchant crewman had never had the gut-churning pleasure of being pounded by an enemy's weapons batteries.

"I'm sure," said Nikolas.

That was when the lights went out in the tube. A moment later, they were replaced with the lurid red glow of emergency strips.

Locklear cursed. "We had to stay on course, didn't we? The captain and her precious schedule . . ."

"Forget that now," said Nikolas.

It occurred to him that they were a little too close to the *Iktoj'ni*'s weapons ports. Those were often the first targets in an encounter.

"Come on," he told Locklear, and headed back up the tube.

"Where are we going?" his friend asked him.

Nikolas considered the question as he climbed. "Up to the bridge," he decided.

"Why there?"

"It's better fortified than most parts of the ship. We'll be as safe there as anywhere."

Besides, Nikolas had weathered a few space battles in his time. If the captain put her ego aside for a change, he might be able to put his experience to good use.

A moment later, he heard the clanging of the ship's red-alert alarm, though the thickness of the tube took the edge off it. *What took you so long?* he wondered.

Kastiigan was on the bridge when word came: Yet another starship had stopped answering hails.

This time it was the *Ch'cheri,* commanded by Captain Callahan. And the vessel's last known location had been directly in the path of the alien armada.

Kastiigan nodded. The report served as a confirmation of everything he had heard, everything he had been given to understand about the situation.

Their enemy was formidable—quite possibly the most powerful adversary the fleet had ever faced. There was no room for caution or half-measures here, no possibility of compromise. The *Stargazer* and her sister ships would either destroy the invaders or be destroyed themselves.

When the aliens' armada appeared, the *Stargazer* would need the best from every member of her crew. And no one would serve more unflinchingly or courageously than Kastiigan. He would do whatever his captain and crewmates needed of him—no matter the effort required, no matter the cost.

He didn't know what the outcome would be, but if Starfleet faltered, it wouldn't be because of him. He would honor the vows he had made when he joined the fleet. And dead or alive, he would make his friends and relatives proud of him.

Ben Zoma whispered two words, "That's it."

They could have continued to download data. However, the first officer's instincts told him it was time to go.

In fact, it was remarkable that they hadn't been detected already. They had obviously stumbled on a part of the warship that wasn't used as much as the others, but eventually someone would pass through and see a bunch of intruders standing around a data node.

And the iffiest part of their mission was still ahead of them. They had to get to the aliens' small-craft bay, commandeer a vessel, and use its com capabilities to send off what they had gathered.

No easy task. Which was why they needed to get about it.

"All right," McAteer said, with a glance at Ben Zoma. *"Now* let's go." And he started back down the corridor, Chen right behind him.

Ben Zoma waited only as long as it took Garner to put away her tricorder. Then he too followed the admiral.

As before, they found the way to the lift without incident. The doors opened and they crammed the compartment, and used its touch-sensitive map to program in a destination.

Four decks down, the doors opened and they stepped out again. But as soon as they did, they ran into trouble.

Luckily, the two aliens in the corridor were surprised to see them. They were cut down too quickly in a hail of phaser beams to get out their own weapons or call for help.

But for all Ben Zoma knew, an alarm had gone off somewhere. That's what would have happened if there had been phaser fire on the *Stargazer*. So he picked up the pace as they headed for the small-craft bay.

En route, they ran into another alien. This one managed to at least draw his weapon before they stunned him. Stepping over him, they kept going.

Less than a minute later, they reached their goal. Ben Zoma positioned everyone except himself and Paris on either side of the doors, their backs to the bulkhead—in case the aliens within had been warned about them.

But as the doors slid aside, Ben Zoma saw that wasn't the case. Neither of the figures he saw standing around the pair of small ships had any idea of what was coming. Advancing into the bay quickly but quietly, he took out one guard with a single burst.

The second one's head turned as the first one went skidding backward, but there was nothing he could do about it. Paris's beam slammed him into the ship behind him, knocking him out.

With a wave of his phaser, Ben Zoma let the others know they could enter. He went straight for the nearer of the two small craft, hoping he could gain access to it as easily as he had to everything else on the warship.

But as it turned out, his all-clear was premature. A green energy beam came out of nowhere, hitting Chen in the shoulder and spinning him around—but leaving McAteer unscathed.

Damn, thought Ben Zoma. There were only supposed to be *two* of them in here.

"Back there!" Paris barked, pointing to the second craft.

Ben Zoma wished he had the luxury of deploying everyone to eliminate the threat—but he didn't. "Horombo, Garner!" he said. "Get that message off!"

Neither of them hesitated for even a second. Knowing he could put them out of his mind, the first officer concentrated on the alien who had nailed Chen.

The rest of the team was already going after him. Ben Zoma took the long way around the first craft, hoping to surprise the alien. But as he came in sight of his target, he saw someone else's beam take him out.

And a moment later, Ben Zoma saw whose it was, as McAteer knelt beside the alien to make sure he was unconscious. Taking note of Ben Zoma, the admiral looked up at him, and Ben Zoma saw the pride in his eyes.

He had contributed. He had made himself useful. He had proven that he could still do the job.

Ben Zoma was happy for him, despite his problems with the man. However, he had more urgent matters to deal with. He needed to know what kind of progress Horombo and Garner were making.

He was circumnavigating the alien craft to find out when he heard a hiss—the sound the bay doors had made earlier. It seemed they had finally drawn someone's attention.

"We've got company!" he cried out.

A moment later, he caught sight of the opposition—and his heart sank. There were at least a dozen of the aliens, their weapons ablaze with green energy as they swarmed into the bay. And there were more in the corridor, waiting at the edges of the entrance.

We're not getting out of here, Ben Zoma told himself, the reality of it tightening his throat.

But they could still complete their mission. They just had to buy Horombo and Garner some time. *And we will,* he vowed.

Homing in on an alien, the first officer squeezed his trigger and bowled him off his feet. But as he took aim at a second one, he heard a cry to his left—and saw McAteer crumple, his phaser falling from his fingers.

Gritting his teeth, Ben Zoma turned back to the enemy and fired again. His burst was returned threefold, one of the beams missing his face by inches.

Ben Zoma plastered his back against the ship and took a breath. *No one said this would be easy.*

Then he poked his head out again and squeezed off shot after shot, not even bothering to follow their results. He just wanted to keep the aliens from going after Horombo and Garner.

And for what seemed like a long time, he did. Not just him, but whoever on his team was still firing along with him, filling the bay with a barrage of ruddy light almost as insistent as the enemy's green one.

Then the situation went downhill—in a hurry. The other red beams were silenced, leaving Ben Zoma's the only one. And there were so many of the aliens, he couldn't hold them off all by himself.

Come on, he thought. *Get that message out.*

As if in answer to his imperative, he saw a beam strike the aliens from the other side of the small craft. It gave them something else to think about besides Ben Zoma. Then came another beam, and another, to which the first officer added some of his own.

It wouldn't make a difference, in the long run. They couldn't take down enough of the aliens to make good their escape.

But the unseen assistance told Ben Zoma something—that Garner and Horombo had sent what they hoped to send. Otherwise, they would still be in the ship, coaxing cooperation out of the aliens' com board.

In a matter of minutes, the transmission would reach a Federation relay beacon, which would boost the signal and send it on. Then it would find another beacon, and another, until at last it reached a starbase.

The com officer there would take a moment to decode it—and when he did, his eyes would pop. Anyone's would, with that kind of gift dropped in his lap. Pretty soon, that com officer and his superior would be opening a channel to Starfleet Command.

It might take a little time to digest it all, and figure out what to do with it, and then send it out to all the captains who would need it. Maybe it wouldn't arrive in time to help everyone, but it would eventually even the playing field.

If Ben Zoma were back on the *Stargazer,* staring at the enemy's weapons ports, all he would have wanted was a fighting chance. Knowing the men and women who served on starships, he believed that would be enough.

There was really no reason to keep firing. But Ben Zoma fired anyway. He just didn't have it in him to surrender.

And in time, it cost him. The first shot he took was just a glancing blow, barely hard enough to make him drop his phaser. But the second one came from a better angle, and it was the last thing Ben Zoma felt.

Chapter Sixteen

BEN ZOMA CAME TO not knowing where he was or how he had gotten there, but he felt as if he had been run over by a starship moving at warp nine.

Then he remembered—the firefight with the aliens, and how they had blasted him as he covered Garner and Horombo. But he wasn't dead. And as he looked around, he saw that he wasn't the only one fortunate enough to say that.

He was surrounded by all six of his companions, in a rectangular room with walls made of the same oily-looking metal he had seen in the supply ship. To that point, only Chen and Ramirez had found the where-withal to sit up, but the others all appeared to be moving in that direction.

Unfortunately, they had been relieved of their

equipment. But then, it would have been unrealistic to expect otherwise.

"Is everyone all right?" asked Ben Zoma.

The others blinked at him dully. However, every one of them eventually answered in the affirmative—with the notable exception of McAteer. Instead, he got up and began walking around the room, running his hands over the walls.

Ben Zoma wasn't sure what the admiral hoped to accomplish. However, he refrained from commenting as McAteer examined each wall in turn.

Finally, a sound of exasperation escaped from him and he said, "Nothing."

Though Ben Zoma had decided not to comment, Paris didn't seem to feel the same way. "What were you looking for, sir?"

McAteer looked as if he hadn't expected anyone to ask for details. "Whatever I could find," he said, keeping it vague.

At that point, Paris too seemed to realize it would be less embarrassing for everyone if he let the matter drop. McAteer hadn't served on a starship in a long time. He had probably forgotten what to do when he found himself unexpectedly incarcerated.

And yet, thought Ben Zoma, the admiral couldn't afford to let the rest of them know that. If he did, he might lose his aura of experience and authority, which seemed very precious to him.

Also, it might undercut his argument about Picard. After all, if McAteer demonstrated an inability to make the right decisions in a tough spot, who was he to judge one of his captains?

"Any guesses as to where we are?" asked Ben Zoma.

"Looks like a storage room," said Chen.

"Yes," said Ramirez. "Probably on the same vessel where we were caught."

Horombo glanced at the door. "And more than likely, there are guards out there. I'd certainly post them if somebody was clever enough to sneak onto *my* ship."

"So," said Ben Zoma, summing it up, "even if we manage to get the door open, we're not likely to get very far."

"Not a very good position," Garner observed.

"But we're alive," said Paris. That was a good thing.

"And together," said Horombo. That was another.

But that could all change, and quickly. As Ben Zoma thought that, he heard the door unlock and saw it slide open. A moment later, one of the invaders stuck his head in.

Like all the others they had seen, his features were hidden by a helmet. He studied the team for a moment. Then he extended his fingers in McAteer's direction and said, "Come with me."

Ben Zoma got to his feet. "Why him?"

"He's your leader," said the alien. He tilted his head as if he were reconsidering his conclusion. "Is he not?"

"I am," McAteer said decisively.

"Actually," said Ben Zoma, "he's the ranking officer, but I'm the one in charge of this team."

The invader made a sound of disgust. He was obviously having trouble with the distinction. Finally he said, "Then you will *both* come with me."

When Ulelo opened his eyes, he expected to see the dark, featureless walls of his cell in the *Stargazer*'s brig. Instead, he saw the pastel-colored environs of sickbay.

He sat up in his biobed, wondering what had happened to place him there. Then it all came back to him—the bottomless abyss into which he had felt himself falling, and the commotion around him, and the sudden, soft feeling of well-being as the contents of a hypospray mingled with his blood.

Thankfully, Ulelo didn't feel himself toppling into a chasm anymore. He didn't see the deep blue forest or the diamond-dust shore anymore either.

All he saw was the facility where his colleagues went when they needed medical attention, with all its stolid, reassuring familiarity. And it felt awfully good to be there.

"Ulelo?" came a voice from behind him.

He looked back over his shoulder and saw Mister Joseph approaching him. Pierzynski was present as well, though he hung back by the room's sliding doors.

Guarding them against my leaving. But Ulelo had no desire to leave. He liked it a lot better there than in the brig.

"How do you feel?" asked Joseph.

"Well," said Ulelo.

He did, too. And not just because his visions had left him alone. He felt clear now, clear enough to talk to someone about the images that had been plaguing him.

Before, he had felt too burdened by them to discuss them with anyone. But he didn't feel burdened any longer.

"If it's all right," he told Joseph, "I'd like to speak with Commander Wu."

Ben Zoma and McAteer were marched along a short, straight corridor, led by the alien who had stuck his head into their cell and followed by two others. Each of the aliens behind them had a disruptor leveled at their backs.

Before long, they came to an open doorway on their left. Their guide walked through it, not even bothering to look back to see if his captives were following.

But of course, they *had* to follow. The aliens behind them ensured that.

There was a room on the other side of the doorway, as large as their cell but lined with observation ports. There were three aliens waiting for them inside. But these weren't like any of the invaders Ben Zoma had encountered previously. These were different in that they weren't wearing helmets.

As they turned to their captives, their faces open and exposed, Ben Zoma got a good look at them. It was difficult for him to ignore one remarkable fact.

McAteer swore under his breath. "They look—"

"Human," said Ben Zoma, finishing the thought for him.

In fact, the aliens looked *very* human, more so than almost any extraterrestrial species the first officer had ever seen. Sure, their brows overhung their eyes a bit, and their ears were small and spiral-shaped. And now that Ben Zoma looked more closely, he could make out shallow whorls in the flesh along their jaws that reminded him of fingerprint patterns.

But that was it.

On the other hand, this group didn't dress very much like humans. It was clear from their coarse leather vests and leggings that their species still hunted wild animals. And it was equally clear from the weapons belts slung over their shoulders that wild animals weren't all they hunted.

But they weren't blustery, in the manner of Klingons. They seemed restrained, measured. And also wary. But then, they hadn't expected to find humans lurking on their vessel.

One of the hide-clad aliens, obviously their leader, stood there while the humans were delivered to him. The other two withdrew a step or two, deferring to him.

Ben Zoma's handlers stopped him a meter short of the foremost alien. The same thing was done with McAteer. The invader's eyes narrowed as he considered them.

"What is your purpose here?" he asked.

Ben Zoma didn't say anything in response. He just stood there. And so did the admiral, to his credit.

The first officer hadn't expected their recalcitrance to be taken lightly. In fact, he had entertained the possibility that they might be executed out of hand.

However, the alien didn't give any sign that he was especially perturbed. He just flicked a glance at his colleague and turned back to the humans.

"Where in the ranks of your people," said the alien, "can we find an individual called Dikembe Ulelo?"

Ulelo was no longer in sickbay. However, he wasn't in the brig again either. He was in Captain Picard's ready room, along with the captain and Commander Wu.

Picard was seated across his desk from Ulelo. "Commander Wu," he said, "says you have some information for us."

"I do," said Ulelo. "I just don't know what it means."

"Commander Wu mentioned that as well," said the captain. "Even so, we would like to hear it."

Ulelo was happy to oblige. He told them of the places he had seen in his mind—the diamond-dust shore and the azure forest and the immense, black plain—and the people he had seen in those places, who looked so much like humans.

When he was done, Picard and Commander Wu looked at each other. "Sound at all familiar?" asked the captain.

The second officer shook her head. "Not to me."

"Nor to me, either," said Picard. "However, if there were humans in those places . . ."

"It leads credence to your suspicion that there are operatives on other starships as well."

The captain knuckled the cleft in his chin. "We should open this up to the science section. They may be able to tell us something about the aliens' homeworld."

Wu nodded. "I'll alert Kastiigan."

Picard turned to Ulelo. "I will need you to tell Lieutenant Kastiigan what you told us."

"Of course," said Ulelo, glad for the chance to redeem himself. "Whatever you need me to do."

He wished he could remember more, because that would make their job easier. But with help from the science section, maybe he could get the captain the answers he needed.

Ben Zoma looked at the alien. It was the last thing he had expected to hear. "Ulelo . . . ?" he repeated.

"Yes," said their captor, his expression every bit as deadly serious as before.

Ben Zoma's mind raced. What in blazes did the invaders want with a simple com officer? For crying out loud, how did they even know that Ulelo existed?

McAteer shot Ben Zoma a look. Obviously, he was entertaining the same questions.

"If I may ask," said the first officer, "why are you interested in this person?"

"I am the one asking the questions," said their captor, his eyes narrowing with what was clearly impatience. "Do you or do you not know the whereabouts of Dikembe Ulelo?"

As far as Ben Zoma knew, Ulelo was still on the *Stargazer.* But he wasn't about to tell the aliens that—not until he knew the reason for their curiosity.

Suddenly, McAteer pointed a finger at the alien leader and said, "He's trying to intimidate us, Ben Zoma. He thinks we'll give in if he's imperious enough."

The first officer had reached the same conclusion. But under the circumstances, he didn't consider it a good idea to rub it in the alien's face.

"But it won't work," McAteer went on, undaunted. "He may think he's the first son of a warrior culture to try to bully a Starfleet officer. But he's not."

Ben Zoma saw the alien's brow furrow. He doubted that it was a sign of amusement.

"Admiral—" said the first officer.

"We're not going to play the game your way," McAteer told their captor, a hint of a smile on his face. "We're going to play it *mine*. I want to know why your people are attacking Federation ships, and I want to know *now.*"

Ben Zoma saw the aliens go stonefaced. Obviously, they weren't pleased with the manner in which the admiral was speaking to them. And if they became a little less pleased, it could cost the away team their lives.

Ben Zoma couldn't allow that. But what could he do about it? McAteer was on a roll.

"What's the matter?" he demanded of their captors. "Not so talkative anymore, are you?"

The first officer put a hand on the admiral's shoulder. "Sir, you may want to—"

"What I *want,*" said McAteer, shrugging off Ben Zoma's hand, "is for these people to appreciate the bind they're in. This is *our* space, Commander. They may have had some lucky breaks to this point, but they have no idea what they're up against." He chuckled. "No idea at all."

The aliens looked like they were getting angrier by the minute, the whorls along their jawlines turning as livid as if they had been freshly carved. But the admiral didn't seem to notice. Or if he did, he didn't care.

"Sir," said Ben Zoma a little more forcefully, "with all due respect, I'm sure we can find a common—"

"A common *nothing*," McAteer snapped. "We don't negotiate with thugs and criminals. We give them fair warning and then we whip their cowardly butts."

It was then that one of their guards raised his weapon and trained it on the back of the admiral's head.

Ben Zoma didn't know if the device had a stun setting or not, and there wasn't any time to find out. Without hesitation, he whirled and plowed into the alien as hard as he could.

They fell together in a heap, but the human didn't take his eyes off the guard's weapon. So when they hit the deck and rolled, Ben Zoma was able to grab his adversary's wrist and challenge him for possession of his disruptor.

He was almost finished tearing it from the alien's hand when he felt something wallop him in the back of the head, hard enough to make his senses swim for a moment. When he regained them, he saw their other guard standing over him.

And the one the first officer had tried to disarm? He was getting to his feet, his eyes ablaze. But he wasn't pointing his weapon at McAteer anymore. Now he was pointing it at Ben Zoma.

"No!" came a cry, savaging the air and echoing wildly from bulkhead to bulkhead.

Ben Zoma turned and saw that it had come from the invaders' leader. He was glaring at the guard, showing his displeasure with what he saw developing.

"First One . . ." said the guard, his tone unmistakably one of protest.

"Desist," said the leader. And as Ben Zoma looked on, the guard grudgingly replaced his blaster in his shoulder holster.

The first officer turned to his benefactor. "Thank you."

The alien lifted his chin, appearing to consider Ben Zoma and McAteer anew. His jaw muscles flexed and relaxed, making the whorls in his flesh ripple.

"You put yourself at risk," he said at last, "for someone you clearly do not like. That is . . . admirable."

Ben Zoma was stunned, but he did his best not to show it. "Thank you," he got out.

"You are not unlike my people, the D'prayl. We too manage to put aside our enmity when blood may be spilled."

"I'm glad to hear that," said the first officer. "Maybe," he added, recognizing an opportunity when he saw one, "we have other things in common as well."

"That may be," the alien allowed. He pointed to McAteer. "Reunite this one with his comrades."

The admiral started to protest. Then he saw the looks on his guards' faces and desisted.

Ben Zoma watched them take McAteer away, concerned for the admiral's safety. But mostly he was relieved that McAteer would no longer be able to get them in trouble.

"My name is Otholannin," said the aliens' leader, "First One of the River People."

Ben Zoma turned to him. "Gilaad Ben Zoma, first

officer of the Federation *Starship Stargazer.* It's good to meet you." *For a lot of reasons,* he added silently.

Ulelo gazed over Emily Bender's shoulder at the uptilted monitor screen, where his friend had put together a picture of a fertile, azure woodland.

"No," said Ulelo, "a darker blue." He pointed to a large, spade-shaped leaf. "And this should be flatter."

Emily Bender made the indicated changes. "Like this?"

"Yes," said Ulelo. "That's it."

The azure forest was the last of the images he had imparted to the people in the science section. The other images were up on other screens, where various science officers were trying to match them with planetary survey data.

No one believed that the aliens came from a world the Federation had surveyed. However, if they identified a closely matching locale, they could learn more about the invaders—and perhaps get an inkling of how to deal with them.

Emily Bender swiveled in her chair. "All right," she said, "I'll see if we've got anything like this on file. Can you think of any others?"

He could almost hear her add ". . . Dikembe?" But this wasn't a friendly visit. It had to remain on a businesslike footing.

Ulelo shook his head. He had described all the images he could remember. "That's it."

Emily Bender looked disappointed. After all, her friend's stay in the science section was predicated on the number of images he could describe. When he ran out, he was supposed to leave the science officers to their work.

Ulelo was disappointed too. Having had a taste of freedom, he wasn't looking forward to returning to the brig. He wished he could stay here with his friend Emily Bender.

However, Captain Picard wouldn't let that happen. Despite Ulelo's demonstrated eagerness to cooperate, the captain still considered him a security risk.

Ulelo understood. It was difficult to trust someone who had done what he had done.

He cast a glance back over his shoulder at Lieutenant Pfeffer, who had been assigned to keep an eye on him. Prior to his arrest, he, Pfeffer, and Emily Bender had belonged to the same circle of friends. Under the circumstances, however, Pfeffer was compelled to put that relationship aside.

He turned back to Emily Bender. "If I think a little longer, another image may come to me."

His friend looked sympathetic. So did Kastiigan, who was sitting at the next workstation and looked up at Ulelo's remark.

"Unfortunately," said the sciences chief, "the captain's instructions were quite specific—when you ran out of places to describe, you were to be returned to the brig."

Ulelo felt his heart sink. "Of course."

Kastiigan regarded him a moment longer. Then he gestured to Pfeffer, indicating that Ulelo's time there was done.

As the security officer came for him, Ulelo turned back to Emily Bender. "Visit me," he said.

"I will," said his friend.

But it didn't fill the hole that was growing inside him. Ulelo desperately didn't want to be returned to the brig. His feelings were so intense that they scared him.

"I can't go back," he muttered.

"I beg your pardon?" said Kastiigan.

But Ulelo couldn't answer him. His emotions were so strong, they were choking him. He could barely breathe.

"Something's wrong," said Emily Bender, her eyes wide with apprehension.

Something *was* wrong. Ulelo couldn't let himself be returned to the brig. He had to find a way to prevent it.

If only I could think of another image, he told himself. *If only I could come up with another—*

"Kastiigan to sickbay," someone said. "We have an emergency here in the science section! Hurry!"

Whatever else was said, Ulelo missed it, because his mind was suddenly full of alien landscapes—not just the ones he had seen and described already, but an army of new ones. A barren, brown valley stabbed by a boiling river. A blue-veined mountaintop sprinkled with black ash. Clusters of red ice exploding in midair . . .

And a hundred others, assaulting him all at once, slashing through his brain like a storm of alien wings.

Ulelo pressed his fists against his temples, trying to stanch the flow, trying to make it stop. But it kept coming, one tableau after another, pushing him to the limits of his sanity.

Off in the distance, someone screamed. It seemed strange to him that someone else should be in so much pain. Then he realized that it was he who was screaming.

For mercy. But none was forthcoming.

Ulelo lurched, staggered, fell. He felt the press of hands, and in the distance a promise of help. But still the images kept coming, a torrent of them, a cascade. And little by little, he was drowning under the terrible weight of them. . . .

Chapter Seventeen

Captain Sesballa stood beside his bed in his sleeping clothes, and listened to his com officer over the *Exeter*'s intercom system.

"It didn't come from any Starfleet vessel," said Ottamanelli. "In fact, it wasn't transmitted by any communication system I've ever heard of."

"Can you read it?" the captain asked.

"I already have," said Ottamanelli. "Not all of it, of course, but enough to know how important it could be."

She had piqued his interest. "What does it say?"

There was a pause. "You won't believe it."

"Do you know Dikembe Ulelo?" asked Otholannin.

Ben Zoma felt that he was building trust. He decided to give a little to get a little. "I do. He's an officer on my vessel. Why do you ask?"

"Because he is one of us," said the alien.

Ben Zoma looked at him, finding it hard to digest the answer. "I beg your pardon?"

"Several months ago, my people snared the *true* Dikembe Ulelo at what you would call a 'shore leave' site, identified through our trading contacts in this sector. Since it catered to a wide variety of species, our operatives had been able to remain there for an extended period of time until an appropriate subject appeared."

"And Ulelo was an appropriate subject?" Ben Zoma asked, trying to understand.

"Yes, because he was of your species. After our operatives abducted him, they again called on our trading partners to transport Ulelo to our forwardmost facility. That was where he was interrogated. But he refused to give my people the information they required of him."

Ben Zoma was starting to get it. "So you sent Starfleet one of your people instead—someone surgically altered to look like Ulelo, who could get the information for you."

"That is correct. And he did. He collected information on your vessel's various systems—in particular, the tactical ones—and periodically transmitted it back to those who dispatched him. And to make it easier for him to deceive you, he was programmed to forget his true identity—to believe that he was, in fact, a human named Dikembe Ulelo."

Ben Zoma's mind raced with the implications. If Ulelo was a D'prayl, an alien had been in their midst for months without their knowing it.

This was getting harder and harder to believe. Then it dawned on Ben Zoma . . . the ease with which the aliens had handled the Federation's ships, hardly taking any damage in the process . . .

It could have come from an intimate knowledge of Starfleet technology. And that knowledge could have come from Dikembe Ulelo, a man the first officer had seen a hundred times and never suspected of anything underhanded.

No, he corrected himself, *not a man.* An alien disguised as one, as strange as that seemed.

"This espionage," the alien continued, "was part of a plan to conquer your Federation and take over its territories."

Tell me something I don't *know,* thought Ben Zoma. "I hope you don't think we'll be as easy to take apart as those first few ships you encountered."

"We encountered no ships, nor did we take any apart," Otholannin explained. "Those who did are members of a different D'prayl subspecies. Its leaders, who have long been known for their aggressive ways, were in power at the time." He thrust his chin out. "But they are in power no longer.

"My own subspecies has chosen not to continue the others' plans. We have no desire to conquer your territories. However, we need to retrieve the one you call Ulelo, whom we know as Rethuin, as he is a kinsman of our highest leader, our First of Firsts."

It sounded like a strange choice for such a risky mission. The human said so.

"My subspecies," said Otholannin, "the one of which Rethuin is a member, is the one that resembles your own. So it had to be one of us who was planted among you. As for why Rethuin was conscripted . . . we still do not know. Maybe because the other subspecies wished to give offense to our First of Firsts."

"So your attacks on our ships . . . have been attempts to find and retrieve this Rethuin?"

The First One confirmed it.

"But why," asked Ben Zoma, "didn't you just ask?"

Otholannin grunted. "Had we parlayed with you, we would have risked the possibility that you would have used Rethuin as a pawn against us."

"Is that what *you* would have done?"

"Were our situations reversed," said the D'prayl, "we would certainly have considered it."

Well, thought Ben Zoma, that's *honest.*

"You can call off the attacks," he said. "If Ulelo is who and what you say he is, we can work out a peaceful way to restore him to you."

"It may be too late for that," said Otholannin. "At this very moment, we are preparing to attack a large cluster of your ships. Until now, we have attempted to avoid fatalities. But in a battle of this magnitude, there is certain to be blood shed."

It wasn't a boast, as far as Ben Zoma could tell. It was just the way Otholannin saw the situation.

"There must be a way to prevent it," he said.

"We need to retrieve Rethuin," the D'prayl replied.

"I can take care of that," Ben Zoma told him. *At least,* he added silently, *I think I can.* "But if I do, I need you to stop your people from proceeding with their attack."

The D'prayl frowned. "It is not my decision. It is for the First of Firsts to decide. But I warn you—he will only relent if he is absolutely certain that his kinsman will be placed in his hands."

"He will be," said Ben Zoma. "I'll see to it my-self. But I'll need a vessel of some kind, and some instructions on how to pilot it. And a few . . . sup-plies."

As Picard eyed the image on the viewscreen, he felt strangely compelled to sit back and laugh.

With more than thirty ships at Sesballa's disposal, the Starfleet defense formation had hoped to enjoy at least a numbers advantage when the enemy appeared. But Picard could see now that even that would be de-nied them.

The invaders depicted on the screen were every bit as numerous as those lined up to oppose them. And of course, they hadn't lost a single engagement yet.

Hence, the compulsion to laugh—which, of course, the captain resisted. He didn't want to spoil what little chance he had of bringing his crew through the battle alive.

"Captain," said Paxton, "Captain Sesballa would like to speak with you in your ready room."

No doubt, thought Picard, *to prepare me for what is ahead.* He wondered if Sesballa was contacting all his colleagues, or just the youngest one.

"Inform him that I will be there in a moment," he said, and made his way to his ready room.

Chapter Eighteen

Picard still couldn't believe what Sesballa was telling him.

"We don't know where it came from," the Rigelian said, his ruby eyes twinkling as he stared out at Picard from the monitor screen in the captain's quarters, "but if it's what it appears to be, we may be able to meet the aliens on an equal footing."

Picard understood his colleague's excitement. The data gave them all kinds of insight into the aliens' tactical systems—weapons, shields, thruster timing, all of it. It was impossible *not* to get excited about it.

Of course, they couldn't trust it entirely, given the anonymity of its source. But Simenon had already decided that it had the ring of authenticity, and no one knew more about engineering theory than he did.

Besides, they didn't have a great many other options.

"Rest assured," said Picard, "we will make the necessary adjustments."

"I'm sure you will," said the Rigelian. "Sesballa out."

Picard sat back in his chair. Suddenly, he was feeling better about facing the invaders. A *lot* better.

"Do you see her, sir?" asked Paris.

Ben Zoma studied the bright, eye-shaped monitor in front of him, embedded in a console covered with serpentine reliefs. "How could I miss her?" he asked ironically.

Unfortunately, the *Stargazer* was one of more than thirty starships amassed in front of them, more than the first officer had ever seen in one place. Under a different set of circumstances, he might have supposed that it was the *enemy* who was in for a beating.

But not now. Not with what the D'prayl knew about Starfleet's tactical systems.

"No one's fired yet," said Paris. "Otherwise, there would be residue in the vacuum."

Ben Zoma nodded. "Good."

They were making their move in time. However, they still had a few small obstacles to overcome.

First off, they were in a D'prayl scout vessel, which—as it bore down on the Starfleet formation—had to have the look of a ship on a very determined suicide run. And they couldn't send a message to their comrades to disabuse them of that notion, because the D'prayl were jamming Starfleet communications.

Worse, their borrowed ship's shields and weapons were humming along at full power, an unavoidable consequence of the way the vessel was designed. So it would not only look hostile, it would prevent anyone from scanning it to see who was inside.

On top of that, the scout ship had a remote self-destruct device—which Otholannin had said he would use in a heartbeat, if he even began to suspect that Ben Zoma might betray him. After all, the First One didn't want his people's tech secrets delivered to the Federation—not any more than the Federation had wanted its secrets delivered to the D'prayl.

Of course, the odds were that Ben Zoma and Paris would be reduced to space dust by their colleagues long before Otholannin might be tempted to use his self-destruct option. However, the stakes were high enough that both Starfleet officers had been willing to take the risk.

Besides, Ben Zoma had an idea.

"We're almost in weapons range," said Paris.

That was the first officer's cue. Getting out of his seat, he made his way aft, where their cargo was waiting in the scout ship's cramped little hold.

It was a roll of the same flat, pale foodstuff that he and his team had discovered in the D'prayl supply vessel. As he wrestled it over to the scout's hatch, which was about two meters tall and a bit more than two meters wide, he was forcefully reminded of how badly the stuff smelled.

However, he had put up with it in the supply ship, knowing what it meant to the future of the Federation. And for the same reason, he would put up with it now.

Carefully, Ben Zoma eased the roll to the floor. Then he swiveled it around a bit, lining it up until its long dimension was parallel with the hatch in the side of the vessel.

Only when he was satisfied with its positioning did he stand up and press a bulkhead control, opening the hatch. Then he returned to his cargo and sent it rolling out into space.

But he didn't let it go all at once. He held onto one end, anchoring it as it began to unravel. Slowly, propelled by nothing except the momentum Ben Zoma had lent it, the length of foodstuff extended itself into the void.

Unfortunately, there was nothing to stop the air in the ship from whistling out as well—a fact that was hardly conducive to the survival of the craft's human occupants.

Ben Zoma would have loved to be wearing his containment suit at a time like this. However, the D'prayl had destroyed all the stowaways' suits in an expression of disdain, long before Ben Zoma and McAteer got a chance to speak with Otholannin.

It was getting impossible to breathe, and cold too. But the first officer didn't dare close the hatch for fear that the ribbon wouldn't unravel all the way.

Only when it had unfurled completely did he toss the rest of it away. It continued to move away from him, vaguely snakelike in appearance, an unexpected ripple against the stars. And as it undulated out there, it displayed something that he had written on it with a dark dye made of fruit juice. It wasn't much, but he believed it would do the trick.

If it was seen by the right person.

Getting to his feet, Ben Zoma lurched for the hatch control and pushed it again. But there was hardly any air left in the cabin, and it was colder than any place he could remember.

Groaning with the attempt to draw oxygen into his lungs, he dragged himself to the tiny port in the hatch and peered through it. The roll was still undulating, slowly and awkwardly, making its way through space.

Ben Zoma bit his lip. A lot was riding on this stunt. He could only hope that his friend got the message in time.

Picard was regarding the enemy, waiting for them to make a move, when he saw a single vessel break ranks and start to cover the distance between the fleets.

"Scan her," he told Gerda.

The navigator shook her head. "I can't, sir. Not without disabling her emitters."

Picard frowned. It wouldn't take long, but they didn't have the time. "Ready phasers."

"Phasers ready," said Vigo.

The vessel wasn't very big—not nearly the size of the alien warships lined up against them. But that didn't mean she wasn't a threat.

And Sesballa would see it the same way—the captain was certain of it. At any moment, the Rigelian would give the order to fire. *This is it,* Picard thought.

"Captain . . ." said Gerda, her normally assured tone riddled with uncertainty.

His curiosity piqued, he moved in the direction of her console. "What is it?"

Gerda muttered something to herself, her face caught

in the glare of her monitor. Then she turned to him and said, "There's something coming out of her, sir."

"Something . . . ?" the captain echoed.

Gerda pored over her instruments. "It doesn't appear to be a weapon. Or a probe." She turned to Picard again, looking more confused than he had ever seen her. "It reads as something . . . organic."

"Magnify," he said.

A moment later, the image jumped a level of magnitude. But he still couldn't make out what he was looking at.

"Again," he said.

This time, the captain saw it clearly. It was a ribbon of something, long and flat and thin. And there were markings on it, too small for him to make out.

"One more time," he told Gerda.

The image leaped at Picard again, looking close enough now for him to see what was written on the ribbon—and what he saw was shocking in its familiarity. A brief series of characters—two letters from the Standard alphabet, followed by a punctuation mark and a couple of Arabic numerals.

CP '32.

What's more, he knew what it meant. CP stood for Chateau Picard. It was printed on every bottle that came from the vineyard where the captain had grown up.

And '32? That was last year's vintage—the best the vineyard had ever produced, if the reports from his mother were accurate. But, beside Picard himself, only one other individual was likely to know that.

That was Ben Zoma, who had heard the captain make reference to the '32 before he departed with Admiral McAteer. Obviously, Picard's friend had a hand in this.

But in what regard? Was he actually ensconced somehow in the alien ship? And if that were the case, how in heaven's name had he managed to get there?

Then there was the most important question of all, the one that clenched the muscles in the captain's stomach and made the sweat stand out in beads on his forehead: What the devil was he supposed to do now?

I know what I am not *supposed to do,* he decided, *and that is to allow this battle to take place. If Gilaad is telling me anything, it is* that.

"Mister Paxton," he said, "get me Captain Sesballa."

"Actually," said the com officer, "Captain Sesballa is trying to contact *you,* sir."

"On screen," said Picard.

A moment later, Sesballa's silver visage showed up on the forward viewer, the muscles in his face taut with tension. And he wasn't alone. The viewscreen was split into six equal sections, each one displaying the image of a different captain.

"If anyone knows what that vessel is doing," said Sesballa, obviously speaking to the lot of them simultaneously, "I would like to know as well."

"I believe my first officer is on that vessel," said Picard, before anyone else could respond, "and unless I miss my guess, he is telling us not to fire."

"The hell we won't," growled Shastakovich, his face florid with determination. "That ship isn't going to get a meter closer without my weapons officer putting a hole in it."

"Frankly," said Minshaya, "I am surprised at your naïveté, Picard. How can you be certain this is not a trick?"

"These aliens have gone head-to-head with us at every turn," said Picard, "and we have yet to win a single skirmish. Why would they feel compelled to resort to subterfuge?"

"Who knows?" said Veracruz, his mustache quirking on one side. "Who knows why they do *anything?*"

"Why are we even discussing this?" asked Nguyen. "It's an enemy ship, no matter what's been thrown out its cargo hatch. It needs to be destroyed."

Picard frowned. "Even if it hurts our chances of beating back the invaders? Or perhaps not having to fight them at all?"

"Why would you think that?" asked Sesballa.

"The aliens could not have coerced that information from my exec," said Picard. "He had to have displayed it of his own free will. And I ask you . . . why would he do that if he wanted us to destroy the ship it came from?"

That gave the others pause. Even Shastakovich. But they still weren't certain as to the right course of action—and there was too much hanging in the balance to take the *wrong* course.

"Well?" said Picard.

It seemed to Ben Zoma that he was floating, twisting out in space like a piece of debris from a ruined starship—or a roll of pressed grain that had been marked with fruit juice, a smelly, makeshift flag of truce.

"Gilaad?" said a voice from far away.

Strange that he could hear out here, in the vacuum of space. Or smell, for that matter. Didn't one ordinarily need air for that?

"Gilaad?" the voice said again.

He opened his eyes and saw that someone was looking down at him. His vision was hazy, so he couldn't tell who it was. Then he began to focus and get a clearer picture.

"Gilaad?" the voice said a third time. And at last, Ben Zoma recognized its source.

It was Picard. And they were in sickbay, the first officer stretched out on one of Greyhorse's biobeds while his friend hovered over him.

What's more, Paris was lying one bed over. They had made it, both of them. They hadn't died on that D'prayl scout ship.

"We know a few things about the aliens' technology now," Picard explained, "so we were able to disable your shield emitters and beam you off. How do you feel?"

That's when it all came rushing back to Ben Zoma—what he had seen and heard on the D'prayl ship. Especially what he had learned about Lieutenant Ulelo. . . .

"Jean-Luc," he croaked.

"Yes," said his friend, leaning a little closer. "I am here, Gilaad."

"Jean-Luc," he said again, knowing how strange this would sound, "we've got to turn Ulelo over to the aliens."

Picard looked at him. "What?"

"Lieutenant Ulelo," said Ben Zoma, "he's one of them. That's why they're here—to get him back."

"But Ulelo is *human*," Picard protested.

"Not according to the D'prayl," said Ben Zoma.

He saw his friend stare at him, trying to digest what he had said. It wasn't going down easily. But then, the first officer hadn't expected it to.

"I'm not delirious," Ben Zoma said. "And I haven't been brainwashed by the invaders."

Picard's brow furrowed. "So you say."

"It's the truth, Jean-Luc."

"But," said Picard, "how do you know that? How can you be certain?"

Ben Zoma had anticipated the question. Indeed, he had asked it himself, back on Otholannin's vessel. And he had received proof of the D'prayl's contention.

Proof he shared now with Picard.

Chapter Nineteen

BEN ZOMA HAD ADVISED that the D'prayl's patience wouldn't last long. So when Picard heard from Grey-horse, he left the bridge and the alien vessels amassed against him, and hurried down to sickbay.

The doctor met him at the door. "Have you found something?" the captain asked.

"Take a look," said Greyhorse, showing him a padd with a still image on its tiny screen—a picture of a white line on a flesh-colored field.

Picard studied it. "What is it?"

"A scar," said Greyhorse, "less than a millimeter in length—so small that I would never have found it unless I was looking for it. And it appears it's surgical in origin."

"Which," said the captain, "would seem to support the story Commander Ben Zoma brought back with him."

"It would," Greyhorse agreed.

Ulelo's internal organs had appeared human on scans. Likewise, his biochemistry. But the aliens hadn't bothered to hide the scars, tiny as they were.

Picard nodded. "Thank you, Doctor."

"What are you going to do?" asked Greyhorse.

"Take the next step," said the captain, "and see what happens."

Ulelo was sitting upright on a biobed. He looked tired, despite the sedatives that had been administered.

"Lieutenant," said Picard.

Ulelo regarded him with what seemed like trepidation. But then, he had been through a great deal of pain, and he had no reason to believe it was over.

"Captain," he said, inviting Picard to add yet another wrinkle to his uncertainty.

Picard frowned. "This is difficult to explain, so I hope you will listen closely."

Ulelo seemed to understand what was being asked of him. "All right."

Here we go, Picard thought. "As you know, we have run some medical tests on you. Through those tests, we have determined with a high degree of confidence that—despite appearances to the contrary—you are not one of us."

The patient's eyes screwed up as if he were in pain. "What do you *mean* not one of you?"

"You are not even human," said the captain, as

gently as possible. "You are a member of a species that calls itself D'prayl."

Ulelo shook his head from side to side. "No . . ."

"It is true," Picard insisted. "And your people have given us what they say is proof—in the form of a code word, which is supposed to enable you to remember who you are."

"No!" the patient snapped, scrambling backward on his bed like a crab. "I don't *want* to remember anything. I'm Dikembe Ulelo. I'm a com officer."

"Then in all likelihood, their code word will not affect you," the captain said. "And it will not matter if you are exposed to it."

Ulelo's gaze was uncertain, fearful. "It won't hurt me?"

"No," said Picard. "I do not believe so."

The com officer still seemed uncertain. "I want to talk to Emily Bender," he said.

It was too reasonable a request to deny. The captain nodded. "All right, if that is what you want. I will ask her to join us."

Bender entered sickbay a little tentatively, joining Captain Picard. But then, she wasn't entirely comfortable with what he was asking her to do.

Picard didn't know for certain that the word he uttered would break down Ulelo's mental block. He had made that clear. He was depending on the sincerity of the aliens—the same people who had been crippling Starfleet ships.

Doctor Greyhorse had found some scars behind

Ulelo's ears. But they didn't prove anything, really—only that the aliens had operated on Ulelo, back when they were preparing him for his mission.

For all Bender knew, the aliens' word would destroy what was left of her friend's mind—and keep Starfleet from knowing what the invaders were really after. Or maybe it would trigger some other response, which would render Ulelo even more dangerous to his colleagues.

But there was also that other possibility, the one in which the captain seemed to believe—that if Ulelo *was* an alien, they would be doing him a disservice by *not* saying the word.

What should I do? Bender asked herself as she approached her friend, Captain Picard, and Doctor Greyhorse. *What would I want Ulelo to do if it were* me *sitting on that biobed?*

"Emily Bender," said her friend as she stopped in front of him.

She smiled. "It's me, all right. How are you?"

Ulelo glanced at Picard. "A little disturbed by what the captain has told me."

"I'm not surprised," Bender said. "I'd be disturbed too."

Her friend looked into her eyes, seeking wisdom there. "What should I do?"

She smiled. "Honestly, I don't know."

Ulelo looked disappointed. But the captain's expression didn't change. Possibily, he knew she wasn't done speaking.

"But," said Bender, "I can tell you what *I* would do, if I'd been having the problems you've been having. I'd take a chance that the aliens are telling the truth."

Her friend winced. "But what if they're right? What if I really *am* one of them?"

That's what he was afraid of! Not the possibility that the aliens were going to trash his mind, or turn him into a weapon of some kind, but the chance that he would be exposed as an alien himself.

And the more Bender thought about it, the more she understood. To lose one's identity was to die, in a sense. And like anyone else, Ulelo didn't want to die.

"Then you need this," she said, "or you'll never be free."

Her friend looked at her for a moment, weighing what she had said. Then he turned to Picard and said, in a voice quivering with trepidation, "All right."

Picard had been instructed by Ben Zoma to administer the aural trigger in a controlled setting. The aliens had recommended low light, quiet, and that no one else be present except Ulelo and the person uttering the word.

And if the word did what Bender had feared, and attacked Ulelo's mind somehow? There would be nothing Picard could do about it. But as he had told Ulelo, he didn't believe the procedure would place him in any danger.

"Ready?" he asked Ulelo.

The fellow nodded. "I think so."

Picard spoke the word slowly and carefully, exactly as Ben Zoma had trained him to say it. Then he waited.

The com officer blinked. *Hard.* Obviously, the D'prayl word had had an effect on him. But was it the effect that Ben Zoma had predicted?

"Are you all right?" the captain asked.

Ulelo didn't answer. He just stared at Picard, his head tilted slightly to the side.

"Lieutenant?" said the captain.

Ulelo frowned at him. "I'm not a lieutenant. I'm a D'prayl. And I want to go home."

It was eerie to hear him say such a thing. And yet, it was the result Picard had both expected and hoped for. Suddenly, Ulelo wasn't out of his mind—he was just an alien in an unfamiliar place. And just as suddenly, the captain had the key he needed to save both sides a great deal of bloodshed.

"I will do everything in my power," he said, "to help you accomplish that."

"Captain?" It was Wu's voice, coming through the intercom.

It had to be an urgent matter if she was interrupting him. He had left strict orders to the contrary.

Looking up at the grid embedded in the ceiling, he said, "Yes, Commander?"

"Sir," said his second officer, "some of the D'prayl vessels are repositioning themselves. It appears that they're moving into an attack formation."

Damn, thought Picard.

"Your orders?" asked Wu.

"Stand by," said the captain. "I am on my way."

En route to the turbolift, he contacted sickbay, Pug Joseph, and the transporter room—in that order. If he and his people moved quickly, they might yet make it in time.

Chapter Twenty

As soon as Picard emerged onto his bridge, he was greeted with the angry visage of Captain Sesballa.

"Where have you been?" the Rigelian demanded. "No, never mind that. Just fall into line with the others. The aliens will open fire at any moment."

"But we agreed to hold our fire until we gave my first officer a chance."

"Obviously," said Sesballa, "that was a miscalculation on our part. Now back off and join the line."

Idun turned to Picard, awaiting his orders. But he didn't give her any. He just stood there, stubbornly refusing to comply with his colleague's instructions.

"Did you hear me?" asked Sesballa, his voice ringing throughout the bridge.

Picard had heard only too well. But he had just

made an offering. He couldn't respond unless he was certain it wouldn't be accepted.

Sesballa turned to his communications officer to make sure the link to the *Stargazer* hadn't been broken. When he turned to face the captain again, his ruby eyes were ablaze.

"Damn you," Sesballa spat, "do as I say—or I will see you stripped of your command!"

You will have to join the queue, Picard thought.

Just then, he saw what he had been hoping for. A wave of D'prayl vessels came about as one, and headed back the way they had come. Then a second wave did the same. And a blessed moment later, the rest of them followed.

One of those vessels would be Otholannin's, with its ever-so-precious cargo. Picard breathed a sigh of relief.

"Transporter Room One to Captain Picard," came a voice over the intercom. "Refsland here, sir. We've got six arrivals."

Picard nodded. It was exactly what he had hoped to hear.

Normally, the doors to the transporter room slid aside as Picard approached them, triggered by a sensor farther down the corridor. But this time, he was moving so quickly that he had to stop and wait for them to open.

When they did, he was rewarded with a happy sight: six figures on a transporter platform. McAteer was there, looking none the worse for wear. So were Horombo, Chen, Garner, and Ramirez.

And in their midst stood a sixth figure—a tall,

darkly complected man with a high forehead and dark, probing eyes, dressed in a standard Starfleet uniform. A man who had been one of them once, and was one of them again.

Dikembe Ulelo.

He looked thinner than his counterpart, perhaps because he had been limited to an alien diet. And there was a spark in his eyes that Picard didn't remember in the other Ulelo.

But beyond that, the two Ulelos looked exactly the same.

Picard approached the man, ignoring his companions for the moment. "Mister Ulelo?" he ventured.

The fellow nodded. "Yes, sir."

Picard smiled. "Welcome aboard."

Ulelo smiled back, though he looked a bit out of practice. "Thank you, sir. It's good to *be* aboard."

Chapter Twenty-one

As Bender entered sickbay, she couldn't mistake the hulking figure bent over a workstation, his long, strong fingers tapping away at a built-in keypad.

"Doctor Greyhorse?" she said.

The doctor looked up from his work. "Ah, Lieutenant Bender. I take it you've come to see Ulelo."

"Can I speak with him?"

Greyhorse shrugged. "I don't see why not."

"Thanks," said Bender. Then she drew a deep breath and went inside.

It was Ulelo, all right. The one with whom she had attended the Academy, and whose company she had loved so much. The one she had believed she rediscovered there on the *Stargazer.*

His eyes opened wide as he took in the sight of her. "Emily?" he said. And a smile spread across his face.

She couldn't help smiling back at him. "It's me, all right."

"I didn't know you were on this ship."

"I got here a few months ago." She glanced at his bioreadouts, which looked normal enough. "How are you feeling?"

"Not bad," he said, "considering." His smile faded and his eyes turned hard, as if he were looking at something the science officer couldn't see. "It was tough, not knowing if I'd ever see anyone I knew again, or if I'd have to live the rest of my life that way—among the D'prayl, in a single room, with guards watching me all the time." Then he brightened again. "But that's all over, isn't it? I'm home now."

She nodded. "You're home." And she put her arms around him, letting him know that his ordeal was over.

But it was funny. As happy as she was to see Ulelo—the *real* Ulelo, who had been so miraculously restored to them—it wasn't the same as seeing the Ulelo she had gotten to know over the last several weeks.

He had been an alien, an impostor. He had pursued an agenda that he had kept hidden from her and everyone else. But even when she considered all that, she couldn't shake the feeling that she had lost a friend.

Kastiigan pushed his food around his plate. He didn't feel much like eating.

He didn't feel much like company either, which was

why he had chosen a seat by himself in the corner of the mess hall. However, a half-dozen crewmen suddenly descended on the table next to him, effectively dashing Kastiigan's hope of solitude.

"So," said Urajel, more than loud enough for the science officer to overhear, "I guess we're pretty sharp."

Kochman looked at her from across the table. "What are you talking about?"

Urajel grunted. "An impostor sits among us day in and day out for weeks, and we don't suspect a thing. Observant, aren't we?"

The others' expressions turned a little sheepish. But then, Kastiigan noted silently, they had all spent a great deal of time with Ulelo. He had been part of their circle of friends.

"How were we supposed to know he was someone else?" Pfeffer complained. "He didn't have a sign on his back."

"I'll tell you what," said Urajel, "he seemed more human to me than the rest of you."

They all laughed at that.

"If anybody else here is a hostile alien," said Kochman, "this would be a good time to come clean. I don't think I could take that happening a second time."

They laughed again.

"Truthfully," said Iulus, "it's a little scary. To think that, all this time, the guy we thought was Ulelo . . ."

They all knew how that ended.

"But now we've got the real Ulelo," Garner noted.

"Yes," said Pfeffer. She looked around the table, a question in her eyes. "I wonder what he's like."

No one ventured a guess.

Kastiigan sighed. It had never been more clear to him that his priorities were different from those of his comrades.

He was glad that they had recovered Ulelo, and that none of his fellow officers had been killed in their confrontation with the D'prayl. After all, they seemed to place a rather high premium on survival.

But for his part, Kastiigan was disappointed in the way things had turned out. Severely so.

He had firmly believed that the conflict with the D'prayl would come to blows—and that he would end up risking his life somehow on behalf of his ship and his fleet. But that expectation had never come to fruition. The science officer had never been given the opportunity to make the ultimate sacrifice.

And he was beginning to wonder if he ever would.

Greyhorse normally didn't like to take chances, but Gerda had left him little choice. Two days had gone by since she lashed him in sickbay over his misdiagnosis of Ulelo's problem. Two entire *days*. It seemed like forever.

He wasn't surprised that she was shunning him, making him pay for his mistake. But he couldn't allow it to go on any longer. He had decided that he would visit her in her quarters, no matter who saw it, and demand her forgiveness.

Months ago, Greyhorse would have been more inclined to plead. But that was before he learned the ways of Klingon culture. A warrior didn't ask for something—he insisted on it. And that was what the doctor would have to do now.

He was so determined, so intent on his mission, that he almost didn't see a couple of crewmen coming around a bend in the corridor. Sidestepping them to avoid a collision, he moved on without acknowledging their presence.

But Greyhorse knew who they were. It was difficult to miss Ensign Jiterica, even with her more stream-lined containment suit. And she was accompanied by her friend Ensign Paris.

He had no time for them. No time for anyone but Gerda.

After all, what did anyone but Greyhorse know about loving someone and having to conceal it all the time? What did anyone else know about intimacy with someone from an alien culture?

With a few more strides, he reached Gerda's door. Then he waited for the security mechanism to announce his presence.

The doctor was about to ask the computer about Gerda's whereabouts when her door finally slid open. She stood there just inside the threshold, looking at him, declining to ask him in.

Greyhorse screwed up his courage. "This is unacceptable," he said. "You will not—"

"I have nothing to say to you," Gerda told him, interrupting him in the middle of his demand.

Then, without any further ceremony, she stepped

back and pressed the pad that would close the door again. Before Greyhorse knew it, he was standing in the corridor by himself.

He felt a pang of loneliness, of regret, of self-loathing. With that as his only company, he made his way back to his quarters, defeated.

Naturally, Ben Zoma was surprised when McAteer summoned him to his quarters.

Not Picard. Not the senior staff. Just Ben Zoma.

He couldn't say no—not to a superior officer. And to be honest, he didn't *want* to. Because if he declined the invitation, he would never discover what McAteer had on his mind.

It couldn't be to chastise him . . . could it?

Ben Zoma and his friend had saved the fleet—and maybe a lot more than that, considering the impossibility of defending the Federation against the Ubarrak or the Cardassians without a complement of working starships. McAteer could hardly criticize them for that when everybody else was patting them on the back.

Of course, Picard had briefly resisted Sesballa's commands. But that seemed to have been forgotten.

Then what was the admiral up to? Ben Zoma was burning with curiosity. Fortunately, he would find out soon enough.

Stopping in front of McAteer's quarters, he waited until the door slid aside for him. Then he walked in.

McAteer was standing by the room's only observation port. His expression was thoughtful, but that didn't mean anything. For all Ben Zoma knew, the admiral might have been seething inside.

The first officer stopped just inside the threshold. "You wanted to see me, sir?"

"I did," said McAteer, never turning from the observation port. "As you know, Commander, I haven't been pleased with the way you and Picard have commanded the *Stargazer.*"

Ben Zoma knew, all right. Everyone did. "You haven't exactly kept it a secret, sir."

The admiral spared him a glance. "No, I don't suppose I have. So as you can imagine, when the *Antares* failed to show up for our rendezvous and we were left to our own devices out there, I didn't have a great deal of faith in your judgment—no more, really, than I had in your captain's."

The first officer frowned at the slight. Why was the admiral telling him this?

"Then," said McAteer, "you saw an opportunity—a chance to help our forces against the enemy. Most officers would have missed it, and I feel compelled to include myself in that number. But you spotted it, and that's to your credit."

Ben Zoma looked at his superior, certain that he had heard the last part incorrectly. Was it possible that McAteer had just thrown him a bone?

"I beg your pardon?" he said.

"You heard me," said the admiral. "You did yourself proud—and I'm not just talking about your plan to board the enemy's supply vessel and stow away when they took on supplies, though that was certainly commendable in itself. I'm also talking about the patience you showed in that cargo container, and the way you carried yourself when you met Otholannin."

This is more than a bone, Ben Zoma realized. *We're getting into crow pie territory.*

"The approach I took," said McAteer, "would have worked nine times out of ten, given the circumstances in which we found ourselves. However, you had the insight to recognize that this was that tenth time, and you acted accordingly."

It's a dream, Ben Zoma told himself. *A bizarre, waking dream.* It was the only reasonable explanation.

"Of course," the admiral continued, "we still had a problem—how to defuse the situation before both sides went at it hammer and tongs. And you found a way to do that too." He chuckled. "Your method was a little unorthdox, you have to admit, but your courage and ingenuity kept us from getting into a fight that might well have devastated us."

Ben Zoma didn't know what to say.

"Which," McAteer added, "is why I'm recommending you for a commendation. Congratulations, Commander." He crossed the room and, with a little smile on his face, extended his hand.

Numbly, the first officer shook it. Then he stood there looking at the admiral.

"Is there something you want to say?" asked McAteer.

Ben Zoma didn't want to break the spell. "Nothing, sir."

The admiral nodded. "Carry on then, Commander. Dismissed."

The first officer started for the exit—and then stopped in his tracks. "Actually," he said, "there is one thing, sir."

"What's that?" asked McAteer.

"An apology, from me to you. Frankly, I thought you had made up your mind about Captain Picard and me. I thought you were so dead set on taking the *Stargazer* away from us that nothing we could say or do would make a dent. But I see now that I was wrong." He couldn't believe he was saying this. "I misjudged you, sir, and I want to tell you that to your face."

The admiral's eyes narrowed. "I accept your apology, Commander, and I appreciate the courage it took to make it. Though given what I've seen of you, I'm not surprised."

Better and better, Ben Zoma mused. *With luck like this, I ought to be at a dom-jot table.*

"However," said McAteer, "it's only you I'm commending. I haven't changed my mind about Picard in the least. I still have every intention of taking the *Stargazer* away from him, considering he never should have been given command of her in the first place."

Ben Zoma felt the house of cards collapse in on itself. "But—"

"In fact," the admiral said in a conspiratorial tone, "when Picard is forced to step down, I had it in mind to make you his replacement. I don't suppose that would be too bitter a pill, would it?"

The first officer clamped his jaw shut until he had control of himself. When he finally spoke, it was in a measured way, with words that had been carefully chosen.

"If that's what you had in mind, sir, I wouldn't bother making the offer. I'm not in the market for a captaincy—especially one that's not vacant."

"But it will be," said McAteer.

"Will it?" asked Ben Zoma. "Is it a done deal? Or are you still planning to go through the formality of a hearing?"

The admiral's expression turned hard. "You know what I mean."

"I believe I do," said the first officer, and he let his words hang in the air.

"You know," said McAteer, "I think I may have mentioned that commendation prematurely. I mean, there *is* a review process. Not everything we recommend comes to fruition."

Ben Zoma knew better. "No problem, Admiral. You sleep well, now. But then, why wouldn't you?"

And he left the room.

But he had to confess that, for a moment at least, McAteer had had him going. He had him eating out of his hand with all that trash about courage and commendations.

But the admiral didn't admire what he had done. All he wanted to do was tempt Ben Zoma into betraying his friend—abandoning him in his hour of need. Then McAteer could say that even Picard's first officer had lost confidence in him.

How could I have been so stupid? he asked himself. *How could I have thought that McAteer was anything but a sniveling, conniving son of a sand flea?*

He couldn't wait to tell Picard about his conversation with the admiral. No doubt, his friend would find it amusing.

Epilogue

EVEN BEFORE NIKOLAS OPENED HIS EYES and got his bearings, he harbored a feeling that something was wrong. And the more alert he became, the more dead certain he was: Something was wrong. Something was *very* wrong.

For one thing, he was stretched out in a bend of one of the corridors, his head pounding, his brow smarting as if it had been cut. When he touched his fingertips to the offended area, they came away with a thin smear of blood.

He had gotten hurt. How?

Nikolas coughed. There was smoke in the air—not thick enough to see very easily, but more than thick enough to choke on. *Why is there smoke?* he asked himself.

Then it all came flooding back to him. . . .

The alarm, shrill and insistent, whipping his pulse into a frenzy as it rang through the cargo ship. The impacts that had thrown him off his feet and slammed him against the bulkheads. Then the glare of sparks, and the smell of smoke.

And finally . . . nothing.

The *Iktoj'ni* had been attacked, no doubt by the same people the captain had been warned about. And Nikolas had been knocked unconscious. That would explain the cut he had suffered.

But he couldn't feel any impacts, so the attack was obviously over. Or at least, no one was firing at them any longer.

Then why hadn't anyone come around to see if he was all right? Where were the emergency medical teams the captain had designated before they set out?

And where was his friend Locklear? He had been right behind Nikolas when they started for the bridge, but there was no sign of him in the corridor.

Nikolas listened, but all he could hear was the hum of the engines. No people sounds, not from medical teams or Locklear or anyone else.

How hard had the ship been hit? he wondered. Were there so many casualties that they just hadn't gotten to him yet? Or were the medical teams themselves among the victims?

Scanning the corridor, Nikolas located an intercom grate on the bulkhead. All he had to do was contact the bridge and find out what was going on. Then he could lend a hand, do whatever the captain asked of him.

Dragging himself to his feet, he realized that his head wasn't the only part of him that had taken a beating. His arms and legs were stiff and bruised, and there was a sharp pain in his ribs every time he took a breath.

But Nikolas could deal with it. Especially if some of the other crewmen were hurt worse.

When he reached the intercom grate, he depressed its trio of red buttons in the proper series and opened a link to the bridge. "Captain," he said, "this is Nikolas. What's going on?"

He didn't get an answer. And a second try got the same result.

All right, he thought, *no problem. The intercom system must have been damaged. I just need to get to the bridge and speak to someone in person.*

Toward that end, he started limping along the curve of the corridor, heading for the nearest turbolift. But he hadn't gone far before he noticed something strange.

There was a liquid dripping down the bulkhead to his right—something shiny, reflecting the glow of the overhead lights. Moving closer to get a better look, Nikolas touched the stuff and rubbed it between his fingers.

It felt like water, but there were tiny particles of something silver mixed into it. He glanced at the bulkhead again, and shook his head. Where would water be coming from?

They did all their washing with sonics. And when they needed drinking water, they replicated it. So there wasn't any water supply that could have sprung a leak.

And yet, there was something watery running down the wall. Resolving to ask the captain about it, Nikolas resumed his journey to the turbolift.

By the time he reached it, however, there was water

dripping down both sides of the corridor, making slowly spreading puddles on the deck. And as he made his way into the lift compartment, he tracked in wet boot prints.

Nikolas expected it would all be explained when he found the captain. If anyone knew the answer, it would be Rejjerin. With that assurance in mind, he programmed his destination into the compartment's control panel and watched the doors close.

Feeling the inertia he had come to associate with the *Ik'tojni*'s turbolift system, Nikolas relaxed. It was just a matter of seconds now before he reached the bridge.

Or so he thought, until the turbolift came to an abrupt halt. Nikolas looked at the readout on the control panel and saw that it was blank, where it should have said BRIDGE.

Funny, he reflected, and punched in his destination again.

But the lift still wouldn't move. And as Nikolas tried to figure out why that would be, the doors to the compartment slid open and revealed the corridor beyond.

But it wasn't a ship's corridor anymore—at least, not like any ship's corridor Nikolas had ever seen. It was more like a subterranean passage, with orange-and-blue cones of hardened mineral drip rising from the floor and descending from the ceiling like teeth in the maw of some enormous predator.

And in the midst of all those projections sat the damnedest thing: a little pond, reflecting some of the stalactites like a mirror. *As if some rainwater had somehow seeped through the ceiling into the corridor and gathered at the floor's lowest point.*

Nikolas swallowed, his throat painfully dry. Was he losing his mind? Had his brain been knocked around in his skull a little harder than he had believed?

How else could he explain his surroundings? How else could he stack it up against what he knew of the universe and make it sound halfway reasonable?

Then, incredibly, he noticed something even stranger than what he had seen already. The cavern's stalactites and stalagmites weren't just standing there. . . .

They were growing in front of his eyes!

It wasn't happening very quickly. In fact, he might not have noticed if he hadn't been staring at the mineral deposits to begin with. But they were definitely growing, expanding both in length and base diameter.

Suddenly, Nikolas heard something behind him. A scrape, he thought, like the sole of a boot scuffing the rough, uneven surface below his feet.

Whirling, he saw that he wasn't alone.

The alien who stood peering at him from across the cavern didn't belong to any species Nikolas knew. He was fleshy, but Nikolas had the feeling that there was a great deal of strength beneath that abundance of flesh. His mouth was a cruel gash in the lower half of his face, showing a few thick, blunt teeth, and the skin of his large, oblong skull was smooth except for a fringe of dark, oily-looking hair.

But what really drew Nikolas's attention were the

alien's eyes. They were glowing beneath his ledge of a brow—glowing with an eerie silver light.

"I am glad you are awake," said the alien, his voice a dissonant jangling of stones. "After all, you are going to be a help to me." He smiled, stretching his mouth from one side of his face to the other. "A *big* help."

Acknowledgments

As usual, thanks are due to Margaret Clark, editor and irresistible force, who every day makes me gladder that I'm on *her* side; Paula Block, Executive Director of Publishing for Viacom Consumer Products, who allows me to write things she no doubt regrets in her more contemplative moments; and Scott Shannon, my publisher, whose support over the years has been so unflagging that I've secretly started taking it for granted.

I'd also like to express my gratitude to . . . well, YOU. (Don't look over your shoulder.) I'm talking about YOU out there, the reader. The *Stargazer* series has been an experiment in its approach to the *Star Trek* mythos, and like any experiment it's been a bit of a gamble. But you've obviously responded to it, or you wouldn't be reading this, now would you? So thanks. And don't forget to pick up the dry cleaning.